Praise for]

"A fine portrait of a heroine faced with true-to-life guilt."
—*RT Book Reviews* on *A Time to Love*

"A gently paced love story with characters who make you care what happens to them."
—*RT Book Reviews* on *A Place to Call Home*

"Irene Hannon wins our hearts with an uplifting story of love and healing."
—*RT Book Reviews* on *Till There Was You*

"Hannon's multithread plot is woven beautifully together to create a tapestry that will enchant romantics of all ages."
—*Publishers Weekly* on *One Perfect Spring*

"Inspiring prose and embraceable characters...capture the reader from the very first pages."
—*New York Journal of Books* on *That Certain Summer*

"Touching, compelling, and satisfying."
—*RT Book Reviews* on *From This Day Forward*

"A great summer read...relatable characters with real-life problems."
—*Radiant Lit* on *Seaside Reunion*

"A warmhearted journey from loss and guilt to self-forgiveness and love."
—*RT Book Reviews* on *Once Upon Nantucket*

"A tender and intriguing tale of heartache, loss, and love."
—*Goodreads* review on *Crossroads*

"A delightful read...the realism and tenderness draw you into the story."
—*RT Book Reviews* on *The Way Home*

"An intense, emotional, thought-provoking read."
—*Best Reads (2010-2020)* on *Child of Grace*

A Time to Love

Circle of Friends—Book 2
Encore Edition

IRENE HANNON

First edition published 1998 by Harlequin Love Inspired as *A Groom of Her Own*

Encore Edition published 2025 by Irene Hannon

(An Encore Edition is a previously published novel that has been revised and reissued with a new cover.)

ISBN 9781970116489

To Tom

My Perfect Valentine

1

"Well, kiddo, this is it." Samantha Reynolds closed the door of the bride's room after Laura Taylor's mother exited to take her walk down the aisle, then turned to face her best friend.

Laura's face was glowing. "I never thought this would happen. It feels almost too good to be true."

"I hear you. But trust me, it's true. And you deserve this happy ending." Sam gave Laura's peach-colored tea-length dress a sweep. So perfect for a second wedding, and for ultra-feminine Laura. As was her bouquet of ivory and peach roses intertwined with ivy and wispy fern. "You look gorgeous. Wait'll Nick gets an eyeful."

Laura reached for her purse and fished out a tissue. "I'm so happy it's almost scary."

"Hey! No tears. Your mascara will run and you'll look like a raccoon. Not a pretty picture, let me tell you." She grinned and gave Laura a shoulder nudge.

A knock sounded on the door, and Laura's brother stuck his head inside. "Ladies, it's your cue."

Sam gave Laura's hand a squeeze, then slipped out of the bride's room and took her place behind the double doors that led to the church. When the organ music paused, then changed melodies, two ushers pulled back the heavy doors.

She was on.

As Sam made her way past the sea of smiling faces, she took a deep breath of the fragrant rubrum lilies. Late-afternoon light illuminated the stained glass windows, which in turn cast a mosaic of warm, muted colors on the rich wood floor.

It was a beautiful and appropriate setting for Laura's wedding.

But the icing on the cake was her handsome, charming groom. Nick Sinclair was a patient, caring, decent man. In other words, exactly what Laura deserved.

She smiled and gave him a subtle thumbs-up as she took her place near the altar, and he grinned in return.

Once Laura entered, however, his attention remained riveted on her.

And at the tenderness and love in his eyes, Sam's throat constricted.

How amazing it must be to be loved like that.

And she couldn't be happier for her best friend.

Also a touch jealous.

Because much as she longed for her own happy ending, that wasn't in the cards.

Her vision misted, and she fumbled for the tissue she'd tucked into the tiny pocket of her pencil skirt. Tried to discreetly dab at her eyes.

But her subtle move caught the eye of the minister, a childhood friend of Laura's.

He arched an eyebrow, as if to ask, *are you okay?*

Forcing up the corners of her lips, she nodded.

The ceremony continued, and when he launched into his remarks, she forced herself to focus on his mellow, soothing voice. Maybe that would keep the blues at bay until the ceremony was over.

While his praise for Laura and Nick was well deserved, what he said at the end resonated deeply.

The road of life *wasn't* always easy or straight. People made wrong turns, took detours, hit roadblocks, had flat tires. But according to him, if you kept your focus on the ultimate destination, you'd always find your way home.

It was a beautiful talk, filled with hope and promise—two things that had long been lacking in her life.

And it was a far cry from the fire and brimstone sermons of her youth.

As Laura and Nick prepared to exchange their vows, she dug out Nick's ring from her other pocket and moved closer to the couple.

But her focus wasn't on them. It was on the minister. Brad Matthews.

The man radiated character and kindness and integrity. And he was handsome. Late thirties or early forties, with silver-touched sandy brown hair and a toned physique. He also wore a wedding ring. Naturally.

Not that a man like him would ever have a remote interest in someone like her, anyway.

Especially a man of the cloth.

Quashing that depressing thought, she shifted her attention to the radiant bride for the remainder of the ceremony. Smiled for the staged wedding pictures. Gave an entertaining toast at the reception. Danced with the best man.

But once all the rituals were over, her spirits flagged again.

What she needed to do was find a quiet spot for a moment and try to stem the tsunami of emotions threatening to swamp her.

She eyed the door to the terrace.

3

It might be cool out there on this first day of spring, but enduring a slight chill was better than watching Laura and Nick gaze into each other's eyes as they danced to the romantic strains of "Our Love Is Here to Stay."

Because if she hung around, the wisecracking Sam the world knew just might break down in tears.

* * *

He didn't have the terrace to himself, after all.

Heaving a sigh, Brad Matthews hesitated as he stepped outside.

So much for a break from the festive celebration that reminded him too much of his own wedding day twelve years ago. The very reason why he rarely attended the receptions for marriages at which he officiated. It wasn't that he begrudged brides and grooms their happy ending. It was just too hard to be reminded time and again that the "after" in his own happily-ever had been short-lived.

Nor was he up to exchanging pleasantries with yet another wedding guest out here in the chilly evening air.

He started to turn away, but when the woman in the shadows at the edge of the terrace sniffed and angled sideways, he froze.

It was Sam Reynolds, the maid of honor.

It seemed the tears he'd detected in the sanctuary earlier were back.

Not what he'd expected, based on Laura's comments about her best friend through the years. Sam had sounded more like the upbeat, irreverent type who always had a firm grip on her emotions.

Maybe that's why she'd come out here. To hide an

uncharacteristic display of weepiness. She probably wouldn't appreciate being caught in an emotional meltdown.

But when she sniffed again, and a choked sob broke the stillness, his ministerial instincts kicked in and words spilled out before he could stop them. "I don't mean to intrude, but is everything all right?"

Sam gasped and spun around, her hand flying to her chest. "Oh! You startled me."

"Sorry about that." He stayed where he was, giving her space to regroup.

A few beats ticked by, and when she spoke she sounded more in control. "No worries. I just didn't expect anyone else to brave the cold. It's pretty ch-chilly out here."

Especially in a short-sleeved lace jacket.

Without stopping to think, he slid his own jacket off, crossed to her, and draped it around her shoulders. "This may help."

"I shouldn't take your jacket. You'll get cold." Her objection was halfhearted at best as she drew it around herself.

"I'll be fine. It was getting warm in there." He tipped his head toward the banquet room.

In the silence, Brad studied her.

Laura often talked of Sam, and physically, he'd had her pegged. Sophisticated makeup, svelte figure, striking sleek red hair. Shorter stature than he'd expected, though. He'd pictured her as statuesque to go with her larger-than-life, cheeky image. Instead, she was five or six inches shorter than his six-foot frame, even in her high heels.

But he'd been way off base on her demeanor and personality. Laura always talked about Sam's composure and self-confidence, described her as the strong, invincible type who was never thrown by anything and never at a loss for words.

Yet the woman who'd teared up during the ceremony and who now stood silent and subdued an arm's length away didn't fit that image at all.

"It was a beautiful wedding, wasn't it?" A bit inane, but it *was* the topic of the day. And safe, in case she thought he was being pushy.

"Yes. Very." She sniffed again, dabbing at her nose with a tissue as she gave him a shaky smile. "Sorry. I'm a sucker for happy endings."

Somehow that didn't ring true.

The Sam that Laura had described might be moved by her best friend's wedding, but she'd hide it behind a flippant remark. She wouldn't cry.

There was something else going on here.

But he was a stranger to her, and the best he could do was empathize.

"I hear you. And this one was special. I wasn't sure Laura would ever risk that kind of commitment again."

"You and me both. But I had a feeling the right man might change her mind, so I did my best to get her into circulation."

He hitched up one side of his mouth. "So I heard. She told me about a few of the singles events you convinced her to attend. I can't imagine she went willingly."

"She didn't. I had to drag her to most of them." A ghost of a smile flickered across her face. "But in the end, she found her own guy. Go figure." Sam tucked the tissue back into her pocket. "You gave a great talk today at the wedding, by the way. I've never been much of a churchgoer, but if there were more ministers like you I might have been."

"Thank you for that."

"You're welcome. And I meant every word." She slipped off

his jacket. Held it out. "Thank you for this too. But I've monop-olized you long enough. I imagine your wife is looking for you by now."

"No." He took the jacket as a familiar jolt of sadness rico-cheted through him. "She passed away six years ago."

Sam's eyes rounded. "I'm so sorry. I noticed your ring during the ceremony and assumed you were still married."

"I am, in my heart. Rachel is still part of my life, even though she's gone. But the ring does confuse people. At some point I suppose I'll take it off."

"You must have had a wonderful marriage." There was a trace of wistfulness in her voice before it turned bitter and her features hardened. "I couldn't get my ring off fast enough."

Brad slid his arms back into his jacket, choosing his words with care. "Laura mentioned once that you'd been married. I'm sorry it didn't work out."

"Me too." She folded her arms tight against her chest. "But Randy was a rat. Sorry to be so blunt, but it's the truth. He walked out on me after only five months and never came back, even though—" She sucked in a breath. Mashed her lips together.

Even though what?

He waited a moment, but when it became clear she wasn't going to satisfy his curiosity he spoke again, keeping his tone conversational. "Weddings can be emotional for the guests as well as the bride and groom. They stir up a host of memories, good and bad. But whatever our experience, Laura is a great ex-ample of someone who found the courage to stop letting the past control her future. And look at the happiness she found."

"Not everyone is that lucky, Reverend." Sam sounded like she was on the verge of tears again.

Whatever was troubling her was a deeper issue than could

be dealt with at a wedding reception. The best he could do was try to momentarily lift her spirits. "I have a deal for you." He tried for a teasing inflection. "If you stop calling me Reverend and start calling me Brad, I'll ask you to dance."

She stared at him. "Dance?"

"Ministers can dance. It's allowed." He smiled.

Her lips tipped up into a slight bow. "I appreciate the offer, but you don't have to do that."

"Don't you like to dance?"

"Yes, but…" Her voice trailed off.

"But not with ministers?"

"To tell you the truth, I've never danced with a minister."

"Well, if I promise not to preach while we polka, will you give it a try? I haven't danced in years, so I'm a bit rusty. But I'll do my best not to step on your toes."

For a moment she seemed flummoxed, but in the end she capitulated. "Sure, if you really want to."

"Let's catch the next number. Maybe it will be a foxtrot." He motioned toward the door.

He followed her in, and when they reached the dance floor, the band launched into "In the Mood."

Sam turned to him with a rueful lift of her shoulders. "So much for your foxtrot. But I appreciate the offer."

She started to turn away, but he grabbed her hand. "Wait a sec. You promised me a dance. Is this number too much for you?" He grinned as he issued the challenge.

"No, of course not. But this is a swing."

"I'm game if you are."

Sam's eyes began to twinkle. "I'm in."

He took her hand and guided her through all the swing moves he could remember. Though he fumbled a few steps, she was an adept follower and never missed a beat.

By the time the number ended, she was grinning ear to ear. "That was amazing. Where on earth did you learn to dance like that?"

"I haven't always been a minister, you know." He looked around and dropped his voice. "Can I tell you a secret?

She leaned closer. "Sure."

"Ministers are just regular people. For example, you may think I dance divinely—no pun intended—but I can't carry a tune in a bucket. However, I love to sing, and it drives our choir director crazy. Susie hasn't yet figured out a way to diplomatically tell me to shut up. She thinks she'll incur the wrath of heaven if she insults me. So I keep singing."

Sam snickered, then shook her head. "I've never met a minister like you."

"I'll take that as a compliment." When the band struck up the opening notes of "As Time Goes By," he motioned toward the musicians. "There's our foxtrot. Can I tempt you with one more dance before I call it a night?"

"Are you leaving already?" There was a tinge of disappointment in her voice.

"Yes. I have an early service tomorrow. Shall we?"

In silence, she moved into his arms.

And as he held her, guiding her through the steps in time with the romantic melody, his heart skipped a beat.

Because it felt good to hold a woman in his arms again on a dance floor.

Yet also different.

Rachel had been an excellent dancer too. But she'd been tall, so they were almost eye level when they'd danced. By contrast, the top of Sam's head barely brushed his nose, and the scent of her hair infiltrated his senses, sending a little tingle through his nerve endings. One he hadn't felt in a long time. And she was soft. And feminine. And appealing at a level he hadn't experienced since Rachel died.

Too appealing.

And too much of a reminder of how lonely his days—and nights—had been for six long years.

Maybe he should have left the reception after the swing. That fast-moving dance had been far safer than this up-close foxtrot.

But as long as he was in for the duration, he might as well enjoy it.

Because who knew when he'd have the opportunity to dance with a beautiful woman again?

* * *

When had she last danced with a man who hadn't hoped a few circuits around the floor would be a prelude to a romp in the sack?

Sam exhaled.

Too long to remember.

Sidestepping those kinds of advances was like running a zigzag pattern to dodge a bullet. That's why she rarely dated anyone more than a couple of times—not because she liked playing the field, as she'd led Laura to believe.

This kind of dancing, however, was heaven—no pun intended on her part either.

And not just because Brad was an excellent dancer.

It was more because of how he made her feel.

Safe. Protected. Respected. Cared for. His lead was firm, yet there was a warmth and tenderness in his touch that made her relax in his arms. To feel as if this was where she belonged.

Unlike their first dance, which had been exhilarating and loud and fast, this one was slow and quiet and more intimate. The subtle, spicy scent of his aftershave teased her nose, and the slight friction of the late-day stubble on his jaw against her temple added an innocently sensuous touch to their dance.

She gave a small, contented sigh.

It was wonderful to be with a nice man, if only for a little while.

And she might as well enjoy it, because it wasn't likely to happen again any time soon.

When the music ended, Brad stepped back and smiled. "Thank you, Sam. I enjoyed that."

Did his voice sound a tad husky, or was that her imagination?

Likely the latter. His invitation for a turn on the dance floor had been nothing more than a polite gesture to cheer up a woman he'd found on the verge of tears.

"So did I. And you've given me a whole new perspective on ministers."

"Then our time together was doubly well—"

"Sam, I've been looking for you." Laura came up beside them, then glanced at Brad. "I thought you left half an hour ago."

"I got pleasantly sidetracked by the maid of honor."

When he sent her a warm glance, Sam almost blushed. A rare occurrence indeed.

"Well, don't sleep through your own sermon tomorrow." Laura gave him an elbow nudge, then angled toward her and took her hand. "I wanted to say goodbye, and I was afraid I'd miss you. Nick's getting anxious to leave."

"Anxious isn't quite the word I'd use, but it'll do." Nick came up behind Laura and wrapped his arms around her waist.

Sam's lips twitched. "Laura, your groom has been patient

beyond belief. Why don't you put him out of his misery?"

Laura's face pinkened. "Will you two stop? There's a minister present."

Nick sent Brad a glance. "I have a feeling he understands. But just so I don't look too…anxious…why don't we end our evening here with one more dance?"

"I'd like that. But I have a bit of girlfriend business to attend to first." Laura pulled her into a tight hug and spoke into her ear. "Thank you…for everything."

At the fervent, whispered words, pressure built behind Sam's eyes.

Gritting her teeth, she squeezed Laura back. She was *not* going to cry in front of an audience. It wouldn't fit the cool, composed, wisecracking image she'd created.

"I'll always be there for you. Remember that." Then, forcing up the corners of her lips, she stepped back and tried for a teasing tone. "Have a wonderful honeymoon, you two. And try to get a *little* sleep."

"Now *that* I can't guarantee." Nick winked, took Laura's hand, and tugged her toward the dance floor. "Come on, Mrs. Sinclair. Let's have that dance so we can get started on the honeymoon."

As they walked away, Sam refocused on Brad. "If you were planning to leave earlier, I must be the one to blame for keeping you here. I'm sorry."

"Don't be. As a rule I do try to get home at a reasonable hour on Saturday nights so I'm coherent for the early service, but after hearing about you all these years I'm glad we finally had the chance to get acquainted."

"Likewise. But if I may be honest, you're not what I expected. I mean, Laura always spoke about you in glowing terms, but my only experience with preachers is the fire and brimstone variety. The intimidating, holier-than-thou type, if you know what I mean."

"Sad to say, I do. I've met a few of those myself. But I'd like to think they're a vanishing breed. And as long as we're playing true confessions, I'll admit that you're not what I expected, either. So we're even."

Though his expression remained friendly and nonjudgmental, Sam's stomach clenched.

It wasn't hard to imagine what he'd expected, after the flirty image she'd cultivated. Most people—including Laura—no doubt assumed she shared more than her time with the many men she dated. So while her BFF may have talked to her minister in a positive light about their friendship, somewhere along the way a loose-woman image had no doubt emerged.

For reasons she couldn't pinpoint, that bothered her.

And for the first time in a long while, she was at a loss for words.

When the silence lengthened, Brad held out his hand. "Good night, Sam. Take care of yourself."

She swallowed, quashing the host of emotions that were deactivating her usual aplomb. "I'll try." When she placed her fingers in his, he gave them a gentle squeeze.

And then he was gone.

The music and revelry continued around her, but Sam's spirits wilted.

Why hadn't she met someone like Brad Matthews seventeen years ago? What a difference that could have made in her life.

But lamenting the past was foolish. With her thirty-fifth birthday on the horizon, seventeen years was almost a lifetime ago. And she couldn't change her history, however much she might wish she could. It was too late for amends, for regrets, for…a lot of things.

As Nick and Laura twirled into view on the dance floor, another twinge of envy nipped at her. Which was wrong. Laura deserved a happy ending. She didn't.

It was as simple—and as final—as that.

2

Sam set two bags of groceries on the kitchen table, pushed her damp hair out of her eyes, and eased off her dripping raincoat.

Too bad the April showers had decided to arrive at the end of March, even if the gloomy weather suited her mood.

Shivering, she crossed to the thermostat in the hall and moved it up a couple of degrees. Hopefully the heat would kick on fast and take the February-like chill out of her condo.

After returning to the kitchen, she fished her mail out of the grocery bag she'd dumped it in and leafed through it.

Bill, ad, ad, another bill.

But she paused at a postcard of a white sand beach and blue skies, framed by brilliant tropical flowers.

Mouth curving up, she flipped it over, scanned the note, and came to the obvious conclusion.

Nick and Laura's Hawaiian honeymoon was a resounding success.

As she propped the card on the windowsill and gazed out at the gray, sodden landscape, her lips flattened.

She could use a little tropical sun herself about now. And with a little judicious budgeting, a trip to Hawaii was within her reach.

But sharing it with a new husband who'd pledged to love her for the rest of her life wasn't. There would be no happy ending in her future.

A fact she'd known for seventeen years and long ago made her peace with.

Yet all at once, the loneliness she usually managed to mask with a busy work schedule and a frenetic social life that was all surface and no depth came roaring back.

Because of the wedding, of course.

Her vision blurred, and a tear trailed down her cheek.

Good grief.

She was crying *again*. As she'd been doing with alarming frequency since the wedding.

This had to stop.

Mashing her lips together, she marched toward the bathroom to get a tissue.

Even a few of her colleagues had noticed her uncharacteristic melancholy, and that wasn't—

Her phone began to ring in her pocket, and she paused. Pulled it out and put it to her ear. Sniffed as she greeted the caller.

A beat ticked by. "Sam?"

At the vaguely familiar voice, she frowned. "Speaking."

"This is Brad Matthews."

Her pulse picked up. "*Reverend* Matthews?"

"The same. Although I thought we'd agreed to use first names."

"Right. I was, uh, just surprised. I didn't expect to hear from you again." She swiped at her nose.

Another pause.

"Is this a bad time? I could call back."

Great.

He'd picked up that she was upset. Again.

At this rate he was going to think she was a blubbering basket case.

"I'm fine. Just a little teary-eyed." May as well admit what he'd already noticed. "I was reading a postcard from Laura right before you called, and like I told you at the wedding, I'm a sap for happy endings."

If he saw through her blithe comment, he let it pass. "Are they having fun?"

"It sounds like it."

"I guess we'll know for sure after they get back. If they look sleep deprived, we can assume they enjoyed themselves."

At his amused tone, Sam arched her eyebrows. "Isn't that kind of a...racy... remark for a minister?"

"Just stating the truth. After all, the physical expression of love is a natural and good part of marriage. No reason not to hope they're enjoying it."

Sam propped a shoulder against the wall. "I have to say you continue to surprise me."

"Well, then here's another surprise. I'm calling for professional reasons. I'm in the market for a house, and I know from Laura that you sell real estate. So I hoped you could offer me some advice."

"I'd be glad to, but I thought houses were provided for ministers."

"That was true in the old days, but things are changing. The parsonage I live in is more or less falling down around me, and the congregation doesn't want to sink any more money into it. Besides, we need to expand our parking lot. So the parsonage is coming down. I don't have to move for ten months, but I decided it might be prudent to start looking now."

Sam strode back to the kitchen, shifting mental gears. "I'll be happy to help you. Why don't you tell me what you have in mind, and I'll take a few notes?" She pulled a pad of paper and a pen from a drawer and sat at the table. "Once I have your input, I can line up a few places for you to look at. Ten months may seem like a long time, but it's really not when you're buying a house."

She listened as he described his ideal house, jotting copious notes. Once she had everything she needed, she set her pen down. "If you have time Tuesday afternoon, I could show you a few preliminary houses similar to what you've described."

"I could do one-thirty."

She scanned her calendar. "That works. I'll call to confirm on Monday night. But don't get your hopes up on this first trip. It's more for me than for you. Seeing reactions and hearing comments helps me get a feel for a client's tastes."

"Understood."

"Good. You can't imagine how many people expect to walk into their dream house first time out. I can't promise that, but I *can* promise we'll eventually find a place that will ring your bells."

"I'm sure we will."

At the hint of laughter in his voice, Sam cocked her head. "What's so funny?"

"Nothing. It's just that you don't waste any time, do you? I wasn't quite ready to start looking yet."

Ah. She'd come on a little strong and maybe a tad too take-charge.

"Sorry. I tend to get carried away when I have a prospective client in the wings. In my business, he who hesitates and all that. Or in this case, she."

"Laura told me you were a go-getter, and now I see what she meant. I'm impressed."

"Wait until you see results before you get *too* impressed."

"I have a feeling my house search is in good hands. You'll call to confirm on Monday?"

"Count on it. Thanks for thinking of me for this."

As they said their goodbyes and Sam ended the call, she glanced out the window again.

The day was just as gray and rainy as ever, but her mood had brightened—thanks to Brad's call...and the chance to see him again.

Which was foolish.

Because no matter how much she enjoyed his company, there was no long-term potential between them. For one simple reason.

She didn't deserve someone like him.

And he deserved far better than her.

* * *

That had been an interesting call.

Brad set his cell on his desk, leaned back in his chair, and swiveled around to stare out the window at the soggy landscape.

Today he'd gotten a glimpse of the Sam that Laura had described for years. Confident, articulate, knowledgeable, and a total pro. It was clear she'd be a great help to him in his house search.

But if he was honest with himself, that wasn't the main reason he'd called her.

The truth was, she'd been on his mind ever since he'd found her in tears at the wedding reception. And while she'd quickly pulled herself together on the phone just now, it was obvious she'd been in tears prior to his call as well.

Unless his instincts were way off, she was a troubled soul—

and troubled souls were a minister's bailiwick.

Yet his interest in her went deeper than professional.

He blew out a breath. Tapped a finger on the arm of his chair.

Bottom line, he liked her. And he was intrigued. Sam Reynolds was a puzzle, with pieces that didn't fit. Just like Sam and Laura's friendship was an enigma.

Near as he could tell from his conversations with Laura, the two women were as different as night and day. Laura had sound morals, strong faith, and a gentle, sensitive nature, while San appeared to be outgoing, flamboyant, blunt, assertive, and definitely not the religious type.

Who knew what had drawn them together?

Yet something had clicked between them.

Until his phone conversation with her today, however, Sam had seemed more like a lost soul than the confident, outspoken, unsentimental, no-nonsense businesswoman he'd expected. And her claim that being a sap for happy endings had made her weepy didn't ring quite true.

He stood. Shoved his hands into his pockets. Wandered over to the window.

The simple truth was that for the first time since Rachel's death, he'd found himself noticing an attractive woman. One who seemed as lonely as he was despite the active social life Laura said she led.

But if she was lonely…if she was open to a new relationship and wanted to get married, as Laura claimed….why didn't she? Why was she still single? A woman with her looks and outgoing personality shouldn't have any problem attracting men.

Brad propped a shoulder against the window frame as rain sluiced down the glass, obscuring his view.

He ought to be working on his sermon for tomorrow, not

worrying about one very attractive—if troubled—redhead.

Yet hard as he tried to redirect his thoughts to the task at hand, they stayed firmly fixed on the woman who'd felt so good in his arms as they'd swayed to the romantic strains of "As Time Goes By."

* * *

Suppressing a shiver, Sam put the car in gear and sent Brad a rueful look. "Sorry to drag you around to three houses in this kind of weather. It feels more like February than April."

"I know." He buckled up. Rubbed his hands together. "Can I treat you to a cup of coffee before we call it a day? Maybe that will warm us up."

He wanted to extend their outing on this chilly Tuesday?

That did more to warm her up than any cup of coffee would.

"If you can spare the time, that would be great. But I've already usurped most of your afternoon."

"I can squeeze out another half hour before I dive back into sermon prep for Sunday."

"Fine by me. Is Kaldi's okay?" A safe, impersonal spot, since informal business meetings often took place at the lively and popular Kirkwood coffee shop.

"Perfect."

Within minutes, they had their coffee in hand and had claimed a booth for two.

As Brad took off his leather jacket, Sam gave him a discreet once-over.

In his cotton shirt with sleeves rolled to the elbows and a pair of fitted, well-worn jeans that highlighted his athletic physique, he did *not* look like a minister.

What he looked was hot…God forgive her for having such thoughts about a man of the cloth.

But she wasn't the only one noticing his good looks, based on the discreet glances being directed his way from women at nearby tables.

He, however, seemed oblivious to the fact that he was being checked out as he slid into the booth across from her.

Once seated, he cocked his head. "What's wrong?"

"Nothing." She took a careful sip of her coffee. "You, uh, just look different out of uniform."

He grinned. "When I'm off duty, I can dress like a regular person. But I think I *under*dressed. Next to you, I feel like a poor relation."

"You look fine." Better than fine, in truth. More like spectacular. "Unlike you, I'm on duty. And this is my uniform." She waved a hand over her slim slacks and tailored jacket. "Dressing like a professional helps build confidence with clients."

"No worries on that score with me. After that third degree you gave me on the phone, I had no doubt you knew your stuff." He leaned back and sipped his brew. "How long have you been in the real estate business?"

"About fifteen years. It's the only thing I've ever done, and it's worked out well for me. Plus, I get to meet all kinds of interesting people. I imagine you could say the same about your work."

"True. In fact, in many ways we're in the same business."

"How so?"

"You devote yourself to helping people find earthly homes. I spend my time helping them find their eternal home."

Her lips twitched. "You have a way with words. I noticed that at the wedding too. Your talk was inspiring."

"I appreciate the compliment, but having to speak in front of an audience almost kept me from going into ministry. I communicate better one-on-one."

She didn't try to hide her skepticism. "You seemed totally at ease while you delivered your remarks at the wedding."

"Good to know. But I'm more of a stay-in-the-background kind of guy. I was on the shy side growing up."

"Me too." The words fell out of her mouth before she could stop them.

Dang.

She'd never admitted that to anyone. Not even Laura.

Brad's expression morphed to dubious. "Now *that* I find hard to believe."

Since she'd already cracked the door, may as well go through. After all, if you couldn't trust a minister with your secrets, who *could* you trust?

"Most people would, I suppose. Shy isn't the word my friends or colleagues would use to describe me. And it doesn't fit anymore. But I used to be an introvert."

"Was there a reason for that?" His tone was casual but interested. Suggesting he was curious but wouldn't push if she backed off.

Not a bad technique for a man who was no doubt used to hearing all sorts of confessions and secrets.

"Yes. I was overweight as a child, and I became the butt of a lot of jokes. Of course that only made me more self-conscious."

"How did you get past that?"

"By being outrageous and funny. Once I became the class clown, my popularity soared. But when I got to be about sixteen I realized that even though the guys thought I was a lot of fun, they never asked me out. So in my senior year I decided to lose weight. I reached my goal by graduation, and my weight's never varied more than a few pounds since then."

"I admire your self-discipline. Losing weight—and keeping it off—can be a challenge."

She shrugged. "It's a lifestyle for me now. But my weight loss had its downside. That's sort of what led to my disastrous experience with matrimony."

Warmth and caring radiated from him. "May I ask what happened, or would you rather not talk about it?"

She dipped her chin. Blotted up a few stray drops of coffee with her napkin.

The temptation to share her story with Brad was strong. His kind, caring demeanor invited confidences and was no doubt a great asset in his job.

She frowned.

Wait.

Was that why he was asking her these questions? Because he'd recognized a lost soul and his ministerial instincts had kicked in? Or did he care about her on a more personal level?

It shouldn't matter, but for some reason it did.

Forcing up the corners of her lips, she lifted her head and tried for a light tone. "Do you have your collar on now, figuratively speaking?"

Brad leaned forward, twined his fingers on the table, and locked onto her gaze. "No. I'm not being a minister right now. I'm trying to be a friend."

Sam's heart stuttered even as a tiny glow lit up the dark recesses of her heart. "Why would you want to be my friend?"

"Why wouldn't I? A person can never have too many friends."

She gave a soft, mirthless laugh. "I think ours would be an

odd friendship. We're very different in many ways."

"So are you and Laura. Yet you two are best friends."

That was true.

And it might be nice to have a male friend. That would be a welcome change from the guys she usually hung around with, who were out for a good time—and whatever else she was willing to offer. "I suppose we could give it a try."

She was rewarded with a smile that sent a little tingle all the way to her toes. "So tell me about your marriage."

After taking a fortifying sip of her cooling coffee, she wrapped both hands around the cup and held on tight. "Randy played bass guitar in a local rock band. He noticed me at a concert I attended the summer after I graduated. We began dating, and within a few weeks he asked me to marry him. My parents were strict fundamentalist Christians, and they were appalled that I was even *interested* in a rock musician, let alone thinking about marrying him."

"Tough situation."

"For everyone, in hindsight. I was a late-in-life only child, and my parents held me to high standards and expected great things of me. But I developed a rebellious streak in my teens that caused friction—especially when I stopped attending Sunday services with them. The day Randy and I eloped and got married at the courthouse was the beginning of a huge rift with my parents."

"Did you ever reconcile?"

"No. And we never will. They're both dead now." She drew a shaky breath. Who would have guessed it would be so painful to resurrect old hurts? "Anyway, to make a long story short, after five months of marriage Randy walked out, leaving me five hundred dollars and a note saying he wasn't ready to settle down and that getting married had been a mistake."

"Did you consider going home?"

"No. I had too much pride in those days to crawl back and admit my parents had been right. So I got on a bus and came to St. Louis, which I'd visited once, and started over. Now you have my life story. And you can see what a mess I made of my earlier life."

"That's not what I see." Brad took a slow breath, his eyes soft with compassion. "I see a woman who's endured far more than her share of pain and disillusionment. I see a woman with spunk and fortitude and courage. I see a woman worthy of admiration and respect."

Her throat clogged, making it difficult to swallow. Even if she never saw this man again, she'd carry a memory of him in her heart to measure all other men against. "You're being kind."

"Honest."

"I've made a lot of mistakes."

"Everyone has."

"Some are worse than others. Marrying Randy was a huge one." But it hadn't been her worst mistake.

That, however, was one secret she didn't intend to share today.

"Did you keep in touch with him after he left you?"

She took another sip of coffee, but it had become cold and bitter so she set it aside. "No. And I never saw him again. About six years after he left me, though, I happened to run into one of the guys from the band while the group was in St. Louis for a gig. He told me Randy had died of a drug overdose a couple of years before."

Twin furrows creased Brad's brow. "I'm sorry for all you've been through."

"Much of it was of my own making." She scrubbed at a spot

on the table with a lacquered nail, but it refused to be erased. "Still, it's ancient history now. My time with Randy seems like another life. The one I have now is far better. And I've tried not to let my bad experience with him sour me on men in general. As I always told Laura, he was just a bad apple. The two of us happened to marry losers the first go-round, but there are nice guys out there."

"Yet you never remarried."

Whoops.

She should have seen that coming.

But she couldn't answer the implied question. So she'd have to play dodgeball. "I guess I'm just too picky." She faked a smile and put the focus on him. "Tell me about *your* marriage. I have a feeling your story is much nicer."

For a second he hesitated, but then he followed her lead. "Yes, it is. Rachel and I had a wonderful marriage."

"How did you two meet?"

"She was an organist at a nearby church, and when the organist at my church was on vacation she filled in. We clicked immediately. We liked the same things, shared a strong faith, laughed at the same jokes. We both loved kids too, and we planned to have a big family."

"How long were you married when she—when you lost her?"

A flash of pain echoed in Brad's eyes. "Four wonderful years. Rachel helped me see the world in a whole new way. For instance, one of her legacies to me was an appreciation of classical music. Her uncle always gave us season tickets to the symphony, since we couldn't afford to buy them on our salaries. We used to look forward to those wonderful evenings out."

"Do you still go on your own?"

"No. It would be too lonely. But I've missed it. I've missed everything I did with Rachel. She filled my life with music in so many ways." His voice rasped, and he took a breath. "Sorry. Even after all these years, the loss sometimes feels as fresh as if it happened yesterday."

"Don't apologize for loving someone so deeply. May I ask what happened to her?"

"A ruptured brain aneurysm. No warning. She was here one minute, gone the next."

"Oh, Brad." On impulse, she reached over and laid her hand over his clenched fingers. "I'm so sorry." Inadequate, but no words would offer sufficient consolation for a loss of that magnitude.

His gaze dropped to her hand. "It was a hard period for me. For a long time I was bitter, and I was angry at God. I even took a leave from the ministry for six months. But ultimately I had to learn to live what I'd always preached—that sometimes we have to accept God's will even if we don't understand it."

Sam shook her head. "You're a better person than me. I don't know if I could ever accept something like that."

"Faith helps."

"Mine obviously isn't as strong as yours."

"So you do still believe?"

She retracted her hand. "Deep inside I still believe the basics. I'm just not into the external trappings. No offense intended."

"None taken. Everyone is at a different place on the faith journey."

Her lips twisted. "My journey looks more like a navigation app gone awry. Except for Laura's wedding, I haven't been inside a church in eighteen years. I don't think I'm church material."

"Why not?"

"Let's just say I've taken a few too many detours."

"Churches aren't for saints, Sam. They're for sinners. If everyone in my congregation was perfect, I'd be out of a job. I like to think of a church as a kind of spiritual app that provides people with the directions they need to stay on course."

Clever analogy.

But not a subject she wanted to discuss today.

"Like I said, you have a way with words. But I think we got sidetracked. You were telling me about your marriage."

"There isn't much more to tell. Rachel's been gone for six years now, and I still think of her every day. It's hard to let go of someone who's so much a part of you."

"Dealing with the loneliness has to be hard."

"More so lately." He locked onto her gaze.

Her heart missed a beat.

Was he implying what she thought he was? That meeting her had triggered a new surge of loneliness?

Because meeting him had certainly done that for her. Except in her case, loneliness was a life sentence. There was still hope for him to find someone new to share the rest of his life with.

"I hear you." She didn't break eye contact.

After a moment, he cleared his throat and adjusted the lid on his cup. "I have to admit I assumed loneliness wasn't a problem for you."

A discreet way of saying he thought she had plenty of male friends who were more than willing to warm her lonely bed on a cold night.

And she had no one to blame for his assumption but herself. It was consistent with the play-the-field image she'd cultivated with Laura.

But she didn't want this principled man to think that about her.

She moistened her lips and chose her words with care. "I imagine Laura mentioned that I date a lot. But just to set the record straight, reports of my promiscuity have, to borrow a phrase from Mark Twain, been greatly exaggerated. When I date a guy, we have a few drinks, maybe go dancing or have dinner or go to a show, but I call a halt long before we get to the bedroom door."

A faint hint of pink crept across Brad's cheeks. "I think I should apologize for my inference—and my preconceptions."

"Don't." She waved that aside. "You came to the logical conclusion. I *am* a serial dater, after all."

"And you've never met anyone who could convince you to give up that lifestyle and take another chance on marriage?"

No.

And she didn't want to. That's why she had a rotating cast of dates.

Because another marriage wasn't in the cards for her.

Before she could figure out how to evade the truth, her phone began to vibrate.

Saved by the proverbial bell, thank goodness.

She pulled it out. Scanned the text message.

"An issue came up on one of my contracts. I need to swing back by the office before I head to a volunteer commitment I have on Tuesday nights."

"No problem." Brad picked up both their cups, slid from the booth, and crossed to a nearby trash can to deposit them.

She stood too, and when he returned she was waiting for him.

"What sort of volunteer work do you do?" He slid his arms back into his jacket.

Not up for discussion.

"It's just an organization I found that does good work.

30

Ready?" She picked up her purse, slung it over her shoulder, and strode toward the door, leaving him to follow.

Apparently he got her off-limits message, because during the short drive back to drop him off, he stuck with the innocuous topics she introduced.

As she pulled up in front of the church office, she turned to him. "I'll be on the lookout for houses for you. I'll text you links to sites I think might be of interest, and I'll be happy to show you any that catch your fancy."

"Thanks. I also appreciate your time today—and your willingness to share some of your history with me." The warmth in his eyes seeped straight to her heart.

"I don't care what you tell people about my ex, but keep the rest confidential, okay?"

"Goes without saying. Take care, Sam."

She watched him walk toward the door in the blustery wind, lifting a hand in farewell as he waved to her.

Then she put the car in gear and continued to her office.

All the while trying to figure out why she'd shared more with a man she barely knew than she'd ever shared with anyone else.

Including her best friend.

And hoping she could find an excuse to see him again sooner rather than later.

Because even if a romantic relationship wasn't in the cards for them, friendship with a man who lifted her spirits and touched her heart would be a welcome addition to her life.

3

What a day.

Brad leaned back in his desk chair and wiped a hand down his face.

A rancorous counseling session with a clashing couple, a meeting with a grieving widow and her children to plan a memorial service for her husband, and a session with the church's HVAC contractor to try to wrap his mind around a bid that might as well have been written in Chinese.

Plus he still had a sermon to write for Sunday—which was only three days away.

If only he could take a short break to clear his mind.

Like an hour with Sam at Kaldi's.

But he had no excuse to call her.

Sighing, he picked up his phone, unmuted it now that his meetings were over for the day, and scrolled through his messages.

The texts were easy to deal with, and he dispensed with them in a matter of minutes. Of his three voicemails, one jumped out.

Sam had called.

As his pulse accelerated, he shook his head at the foolish reaction. This was no doubt a business call.

But just hearing her voice would be a welcome pick-me-up.

He put the phone on speaker and played back the message.

"Hi, Brad. Sorry to bother you in the middle of a workday. I'm sure you're super busy. But a corporate client just offered me two tickets to the symphony for tomorrow night and I thought of you. I know it's short notice, and I realize you may not want to go back there without Rachel, but if you're interested let me know. Hope all is well."

As warmth effervesced through him, his gaze fell on the picture of Rachel that had graced his bookcase for almost a decade.

A sudden niggle of guilt made the effervescence go slightly flat.

Somehow it felt disloyal to look forward to spending time in the company of another woman.

Expelling a breath, he rose and crossed to the bookcase. Picked up the picture and studied the face of the woman who had captured his heart with her gentleness and grace and goodness, and who would always hold a special place there.

They'd been too young and had felt too invincible ever to discuss the kind of tragedy that had befallen them, but if the situation were reversed he would have wanted her to find someone else to share her life with. Someone who would let her give expression to her bountiful love.

And with her caring heart and loving nature, she would want him to do the same.

Not that Sam was a candidate for that role, of course. Theirs could never be more than a friendship. Even if she wasn't quite the party girl he'd assumed her to be, they were too different for anything serious to develop. But a meet-up for coffee or a trip to the symphony could be a first, safe step back into the social world.

Gently he placed the picture back on the bookcase. Then he retraced his steps to his desk and returned Sam's call.

33

She answered on the second ring. "Hi there. I hope my earlier call didn't interrupt your day."

"Only in the best possible way. I appreciate the invitation."

"To be honest, I wasn't sure I should ask you. I didn't want to stir up sad memories."

"My symphony memories are all happy. Going back alone would have been melancholy, but I'm up for it with you."

A beat ticked by.

"Is that a yes?" She sounded surprised.

"It is."

"Great. The concert starts at seven-thirty, so we could either meet there or I could pick you up."

"Why don't I pick *you* up? Since you supplied the tickets, the least I can do is provide the transportation."

"Well, if you're sure, that would be fine."

"I've got a four-thirty appointment tomorrow, so would six be okay?"

"That works. Let me give you the access code to the lobby of my condo." She recited the numbers.

"Got it. Now all I need is an address and unit number." He jotted down the information she provided. "Okay. I'll see you at six tomorrow. Thank you again for thinking of me."

"To be honest, you were the first person who came to mind. Most of the men in my acquaintance are more into sports than Schubert." There was a wry note in her voice.

"My gain, their loss. I'll see you tomorrow."

Once they said their goodbyes, Brad leaned back in his chair. Weighed the phone in his hand as he tried to rein in the grin tugging at his lips and the little trill of excitement that was making his fingertips tingle.

After all, there was no reason to think there was anything

personal in Sam's invitation. Nor did he want there to be. But a friend, he could use.

Funny.

At the wedding, he'd sought her out because *she* seemed to need a friend.

But as he'd discovered, he needed one too. Especially one who'd prompt him to do things he'd put off far too long. Like go out for a coffee date and get back on the dance floor and attend a concert.

In other words, to start to live again.

Brad smiled and turned toward his laptop to work on his sermon.

God really did work in mysterious ways.

And often through the most unexpected vessels.

* * *

Sam stared at her reflection in the full-length mirror. Frowned.

While her silk blouse and pearls were demure, her skirt was on the short side. But there'd been no other option. Short was her go-to length, so the choices in her closet were either short or shorter. But maybe she should have toned down her makeup. Gone for a less dramatic effect. After all, she was spending the evening with a minister.

She blew out a breath.

This was silly.

Why was she worrying about stuff that didn't matter? This wasn't a date, after all. Far from it. This was nothing more than one friend inviting another to enjoy the largesse of a client.

Somehow her heart didn't get that message, though, because when the doorbell rang a moment later her pulse skittered.

How dumb was that?

Rolling her eyes, she tugged on her skirt to try to eke out another half-inch of length, walked to the door, and pulled it open.

Brad gave her a quick head-to-toe, and if she didn't know better she'd have sworn the warmth in his eyes was more than friendly when his gaze met hers.

"You look very nice."

"Thanks. So do you." No lie there. His dove-gray suit, white shirt, and silk tie were more suited to a man of the world than a man of the cloth, and the faint brush of silver at his temples added a distinguished—and appealing—touch. Stepping back, she motioned him through the door. "Come on in. I'll be ready to leave as soon as I get my sweater."

"No rush. We should have plenty of time to get there." He strolled into the foyer, pausing on the threshold of the living room to give the décor a sweep. "Impressive. I feel like I've stepped into the pages of a decorating magazine."

Her scan was more indifferent.

The white walls, light gray modular furniture, glass-and-chrome coffee and end tables, and black fireplace screen were the definition of neutral. Throw pillows in magenta and cobalt blue added the only touch of color.

"Thanks. It's functional, and it suits my lifestyle. But I wouldn't call it homey."

"It doesn't seem like homey was what you were after." He studied her with those perceptive eyes of his.

"That's true." Not that she'd ever thought about it before, or analyzed her decorating choices. But the contemporary, picture-perfect room was more like a stage setting. A backdrop for a single, socializing, professional woman rather than a home.

"So is this the real you?" Brad swept a hand over the room.

"No. I mean, I do have contemporary tastes. So the old Victorian Nick and Laura bought, charming as it is, wouldn't be my style. If I was decorating this room for a family, it would include homey touches to warm it up."

"Like what?"

"Like a handloomed throw on that sofa." She motioned to the modular couch. "Maybe a needlepoint pillow next to the fireplace. A vase of flowers from my own garden. A child's drawing framed and hung on the wall." Her voice rasped, and she cleared her throat.

Dang.

How did this man dredge up yearnings she thought she'd long ago tamed?

"I have to believe you could have all that if you wanted it. You're an intelligent, beautiful woman." Brad's voice was quiet as he scrutinized her with a probing look that suggested he was perhaps seeing more than she wanted to reveal.

Flattered as she was by his compliment, the truth was, there was no family in her future. She'd had her chance once, and she'd thrown it away. That's why it was better to live in a more sterile environment, where she could more easily pretend that those things were unimportant to her.

But none of that was on the agenda for tonight's conversation.

She pasted on a bright smile. "Maybe someday. Let me grab my sweater." Then she fled to the bedroom.

When she rejoined him, she changed the subject to real estate, using the drive downtown to talk about her search for a house for him.

And once the concert started, there was no further need for conversation.

As music filled the air around her, she sank back in the plush seat and let the strains of Vaughan Williams's "The Lark Ascending" wash over her. The music was beautiful, but hard as she tried, it was impossible to relax with Brad's sleeve brushing her arm whenever he moved, the faint hint of his tantalizing cologne teasing her nose, and his potent masculinity invading her space.

When she peeked over at him a few times during the concert, he seemed engrossed in the performance. But now and then, faint furrows dented his brow.

Perhaps he was remembering happier times here with Rachel.

Shoot.

Maybe this would end up being a downer evening for him.

When the lights came up for intermission, she angled toward him. "The music is great, but I hope being here again isn't making you too sad."

"It's a little bittersweet. But Rachel wouldn't have wanted me to stop doing something I love. I've thought about coming back here, but it took your invitation to make me pull the trigger. I owe you for that."

She called up a smile. "What are friends for, right?"

A beat ticked by as an odd expression flitted across his face. "Right. So when was the last time *you* were here?"

"I came once last year. Gratis tickets again, with Laura as my date. Like I said, the guys I date aren't into the culture scene."

"This guy is."

"Except we aren't on a legit date."

Another beat ticked by. "No, I suppose not."

She squinted at him. He almost sounded sorry they weren't.

But surely she was reading too much into the faint nuances in his inflection and expression.

Best to keep their banter lighthearted.

"Of course not. What kind of minister would date a woman who wears short skirts and lays on makeup this thick?" She waved a hand over herself.

He flicked a glance at her skirt and frowned. "For the record, I don't consider your skirt too short. And I'm no expert on makeup, but I think you look great."

Huh.

Maybe her appearance wasn't as off-putting as she'd expected.

"You know, you really are dismantling my stereotype of preachers."

His lips quirked. "From what you've said about your image of my vocation, I consider that a good thing."

"Laura never told me you were so…I don't know. Approachable and down-to-earth." Not to mention handsome and appealing.

"Would that have tempted you to come to a service at my church and see me in action?" A twinkle appeared in his eyes.

"Maybe."

"It's not too late. You'd be welcome any Sunday."

"I'll have to think about that." Because a person should go to church to commune with God, not to ogle the minister. But in truth, if all of Brad's sermons were as uplifting and thought-provoking as the talk he'd given at the wedding, that could be sufficient reason to attend. Plus, a bit of spirituality might help fill the empty places in her life.

"Speaking of Laura—when are they getting back from Hawaii?" Brad adjusted his tie.

"This weekend. She and I are having lunch next week."

"The two of you seem to be very close. How did you meet?"

Sam wrinkled her nose. "Believe it or not, in the ladies' room at the junior college where we were both taking classes. Not the most auspicious beginning. But she seemed in need of a friend, and I was available. I found out later that her life was pretty awful at that point. I'm sure if she hadn't been so desperate she would have been a little more choosy about who she associated with."

Brad's brow puckered. "Don't sell yourself short. Laura's an excellent judge of character. She wouldn't hang out with someone who wasn't a good person."

At the misplaced compliment, Sam's stomach twisted.

Nevertheless, she managed to prop up the corners of her mouth. "You're giving me too much credit."

"I don't think so. And I doubt Laura would, either."

Maybe not.

But Laura didn't know her best friend's darkest secret, either.

Pressure built behind Sam's eyes, and she dipped her chin on the pretext of tucking her program under the purse on her lap. Time to change the subject. "Speaking of good people, tell me how you decided to become a minister."

The low buzz of conversation around them seemed to intensify as he regarded her with those discerning eyes of his.

She'd have to continue to deflect if he pressed for more information about her last comment.

Thankfully, he took her cue. "I think I always knew this was what I was meant to do. I grew up in a house where Christian values were not only taught, but lived. And unlike you, I knew a couple of ministers who were down-to-earth and humble, and who seemed to find great satisfaction in their work. I also like helping people, and being a minister allows me to spend my life doing that."

"It's hard getting involved in people's problems, though,

isn't it?" As she knew from her weekly stint at the counseling center. "I mean, you can't help everyone who comes to you."

"True. And that's tough. Rachel always said I needed to learn how to compartmentalize, for my own mental health, but I've never quite gotten the hang of it."

"Taking time for fun once in a while could help."

"I was better at that when Rachel was here. Before she came into my life, I was a pretty serious guy."

"Past tense?" Sam arched an eyebrow at him.

His lips twisted into a rueful grin. "Touché. But I think being serious goes with the job. However, I used to give myself a break from work now and then. Not much in the past few years, but maybe I'm making a new start tonight."

Sam tapped her finger on the arm of her chair.

It was obvious the man sitting beside her had enjoyed being married, and that having a wife had added much-needed balance to his life. Plus, after having such a wonderful marriage, he had to be lonely. A new relationship could do wonders for him.

Not with her, of course.

That would be absurd.

But he was kind, considerate, empathetic, attractive, a great conversationalist. In other words, the kind of man any woman would be drawn to. If he could meet a few who were eligible.

Hmm.

She knew some nice, single women. Setting up an introduction or two would be the unselfish thing to do. Even if the thought of him seeing other women left an unpleasant feeling in the pit of her stomach.

"What are you thinking?" He gave her a quizzical look.

She took a deep breath and plunged in before she got cold feet. "Speaking of new starts, I think you should dip your toes back into the dating scene. There's nothing like romance to perk up your life. Just ask Laura. And if you found another woman to love, it would be easier to curb your workaholic tendencies and add more fun to your life."

Brad stared at her. "You don't beat around the bush, do you?"

She hiked up one shoulder. "I call 'em like I see 'em—as I'm sure Laura told you."

His lips flexed. "Yes. I believe the word blunt has come up in conversations about you. And I do appreciate honesty. But I'm not sure I'm ready for anything beyond friendship with a woman. For one thing, I'm rusty on the finer points of dating. Rachel was the only woman I ever went out with, and that was a long time ago."

"I can see how it could be kind of scary to date again after such a long time, but you have to start sooner or later—assuming you're open to the possibility of another relationship, of course."

He took a deep breath. "I'm getting there."

"In that case, I know a perfect woman for you to take out. She's on the quiet side, refined, likes music and books. She hasn't dated much, either, so she'll probably be just as nervous as you are. That will level the playing field. Why don't you let me give her a call and see if she's interested? You don't have anything to lose by going on one date."

He played with the edge of his program, faint furrows creasing his brow. "I guess that's true."

Sam's spirits dipped, but she managed to hold onto her smile. "I'll touch base with her tomorrow. Her name's Stephanie Morris, and she's a librarian."

A hint of humor flared in his irises. "I can see that no grass grows under *your* feet. First you get me out house-hunting before I'd planned to pull the trigger, and now you're lining up dates for me. I'm beginning to wonder what's next."

"You never know with Sam Reynolds. Just ask Laura."

"I might. But you have to promise me one thing. No singles bars."

Sam snuffled. "Don't worry. I wouldn't even think about it. I can't picture you in one of those places."

"I can't picture Laura in one, either, and you managed to get her to a few."

"Kicking and screaming. Come to think of it, though…the night we ran into Nick in one seemed to be a turning point in their relationship."

"Sam." He gave her a warning look. "Don't get any ideas."

At the hint of panic in his eyes, she forced another smile. "Don't worry. You're safe with me."

The orchestra began tuning up, signaling the end of the intermission, and she angled back toward the stage. Fought back a surge of melancholy.

Setting Brad up was a considerate thing to do. It was obvious he was lonely, and Stephanie was a nice woman. The two of them were well-suited to each other, as far as she could see. And since Brad had gone out of his way to be kind to her at the wedding, she ought to do something to brighten his life in return.

Even if the thought of sending him off to another woman made her want to cry.

4

O h, for heaven's sake.

April was supposed to bring showers, not monsoons.

Sam dashed into the café where she and Laura had agreed to meet, pausing inside the door as her umbrella dripped and the hostess gave the growing puddle on the floor an annoyed glance.

Tough.

She'd had her own challenging morning. Like dodging raindrops with two different clients, both of whom lingered far longer than expected at every house, plus maneuvering through a major traffic jam. All of which had conspired to make her twenty minutes late for her lunch date.

Holding her umbrella at arm's length, she moved to the mirror in the lobby and peered at her reflection. Winced.

She not only *felt* frazzled, she *looked* frazzled.

After trying to finger-comb her hair, she relegated her do to the lost-cause category.

Thank goodness there were no client meetings on her afternoon agenda. Only paperwork.

She moved to the doorway of the dining room and gave it a scan, homing in on Laura. Her best friend was seated at a quiet corner table, sipping a cup of tea, looking placid and dreamy-eyed.

The aftereffect of a perfect honeymoon, no doubt.

Laura didn't see her until she drew close, then beamed her a warm smile. "You made it. Your text sounded a bit crazed. I was afraid you got washed away in this deluge."

"Not quite." Sam slid into the facing seat. "Sorry again for the delay, kiddo. You won't believe the morning I had." She gave her a rapid recap.

"Wow. No wonder you look stressed-out. Do you want a cup of tea? Or would you prefer something stronger?"

"Stronger would be great, but I'm on duty. Tea will have to do. And I'll have whatever kind you're drinking. It seems to have a relaxing effect."

Laura's lips bowed. "I think my state of mind has more to do with three weeks in Hawaii."

"I had a feeling that might be the case." She studied her. The fine lines of tension that had always been around her eyes were gone, and the faint, parallel etchings on her brow had all but disappeared. "I don't think I've ever seen you look this mellow."

"It's been years since I *felt* this mellow. Nick is so amazing. Sometimes I still can't believe he said 'I do.'"

"Trust me, he said it. I'm your witness—literally. So tell me everything. Well…almost everything." She winked.

Laura was happy to comply, face animated, eyes filled with the awe of new love as they ate their lunch.

And Sam couldn't be happier for her. Laura deserved a happy ending after her traumatic first marriage and subsequent years of guilt and loneliness. It had taken a special man to help her overcome her fear of commitment and find the courage to take a second chance on love, but Nick had been worth waiting for

"And so it was super hard to come back." Laura didn't wrap up until they were finishing dessert. "I don't think anyone ever had such a perfect honeymoon."

"I won't argue with that, not after all your stories. I'll have to tell Brad that his theory about judging how much fun you had by how sleep deprived you looked was wrong."

Laura's brow bunched. "Brad who?"

"Matthews. Your minister."

Laura still looked confused. "When did Brad say this? At the wedding?"

"No. On the phone afterward. He called me because they're going to tear the parsonage down and he needs to find a house. He said you told him I was in real estate, and he thought I could help." Sam ate another spoonful of her chocolate mousse.

"That makes sense. I'd forgotten about the parsonage situation. I'm glad he's taking advantage of your expertise."

"You know, I'm surprised you and he never clicked."

Laura's face went blank. "You mean romantically?"

"Sure. Why not?"

"I grew up with him, Sam. He was more like a brother. And when he became a minister, I started thinking of him in that role. Besides, he was married until six years ago, and at that point the last thing on my mind was romance. Even if it had been, competing with a wife who was deeply loved would be a challenge."

"I hear you. It sounds like Rachel was a wonderful person."

Laura cocked her head. "Did Brad tell you about her?"

"A little. The subject came up during our phone conversation, and again when we stopped for coffee."

"Wait a minute." Laura set her teacup down. "You and Brad had a coffee date?"

"No. It wasn't a date. After I took him out to look at a few houses on a cold day, we stopped for a warm-up."

"But how did you get him to talk about Rachel? I've always gotten the impression the subject was too painful for him to discuss. I mean, her death was such a tragedy."

"I know. I'm not certain why he talked about her to me, except he seems lonely and I'm not a bad listener. Maybe he just needed a sounding board. Sometimes people have to talk things through before they can let them go, and I think he's trying to move on. Why else would he have agreed to the blind date I suggested after the symphony?"

Laura's eyes rounded. "You went to the symphony with Brad? And he's going on a blind date?"

Uh-oh.

Maybe she'd spilled too much.

"Yes to both, but he may not want anyone to know about the date, so keep it to yourself."

"Of course. What about the symphony?"

She gave a dismissive wave and kept her tone casual. "I got free tickets and invited him, since you were otherwise occupied in Hawaii. Plus, Brad had mentioned that he and Rachel used to enjoy going."

"That was kind of you."

"Why not share the largesse? He's a nice man. Head and shoulders above most of the guys in my circle."

"I agree that it would be hard to find many guys nicer than Brad." Laura picked up her teacup again. "It's just that I would never have paired you two up."

"Whoa." She held up a hand, palm forward. "That's way too strong a term. We have the beginning of a friendship, nothing more. Although why in heaven's name—pardon the ecclesiastical reference—someone like Brad would be interested in having a friend like me is a puzzle. We're very different."

"So are you and I, and we're best buds."

"Brad pointed that out when I raised the issue."

Laura studied her. "So you enjoy being in his company?"

"Sure. I mean, what's not to like? He's smart, kind, empathetic, and intelligent. And he has a good sense of humor."

"He's not too hard on the eyes, either." Laura took a sip of tea, watching her over the rim.

"Hey. Let's give credit where credit is due. I'm sorry if it's in bad taste to say this about a minister, but he's hot. Not that I'm interested in him in that way, of course. Can you imagine swinging single Sam and straight-arrow minister Brad? Not a good fit. Besides, I'm not in the market for romance at the moment."

"Since when?" Laura's eyebrows peaked. "I thought you were always looking for Mr. Right."

"Not anymore, kiddo. I've called a moratorium on the search. I'm just glad you found your Prince Charming."

"But why did you stop looking? For as long as I've known you, you've been on the hunt for a husband."

"Things change." And that was all she was going to say about that. There was no way she'd ever tell Laura that her husband hunt had been a ploy to try to convince her best friend to give marriage a second go. It was time to move on to a new topic. "Before I forget, I have a favor to ask."

"Name it."

"Don't fall off your chair, but I was wondering if I could go with you sometime to one of your Bible study classes."

Laura's jaw dropped.

No surprise there.

Truth be told, she'd felt sort of the same way when the idea occurred to her out of the blue, right after she and Brad had gone out for coffee.

But if a man like him had chosen to make ministry his life's work, and if someone like Laura had found enough strength in her faith to carry her through the traumatic years of her marriage and the hardships that followed, maybe it was worth checking out.

Assuming Laura ever got over her shock.

Sam leaned over and waved her hand in front of her lunch partner's face. "Hello? Is anybody home?"

Laura inhaled. "I'm here. Just surprised. Of course you can come with me. We meet on Thursday from seven-thirty to nine."

"And this is a group of people from all over the area, right? Not just Brad's congregation."

"Right."

"And it's not at Brad's church?"

"No."

"Okay. I'll give it a shot. But don't say anything about this to anyone. Until I know if it's going to work out, I'd rather keep it quiet."

"You're going to tell Brad, aren't you?"

"No. Not yet, anyway. Heck, I might only last one session." Sam grinned, then glanced at her watch. "You may be a lady of leisure for a few more days, but some of us aren't so lucky." She slung her purse over her shoulder and reached across the table to squeeze Laura's hand. "I'm glad you had such a wonderful time. You deserve it. Give Nick my best, and let's talk soon."

"Count on it." The speculative gleam in her friend's eyes was impossible to miss.

"This will cover my lunch." Sam pulled out her wallet, extracted a bill, and laid it on the table. "Will you settle up?"

"No problem. And Sam...I'm glad you and Brad connected."

"We're friends, Laura. Remember, I'm setting him up with someone else for a date."

"Right." But the twinkle in her eyes didn't dim.

Oh, brother.

The last thing she needed was her best friend getting any ideas that would lead nowhere.

Especially since she had enough for the both of them.

* * *

"Hi, Sam. Listen, I have a huge favor to ask."

As Laura's voice came over her cell several days later, Sam continued scanning the seller's disclosure on the house she'd just listed. "I'll help if I can. What's up?"

"I'm in charge of a program at our church that puts on practical seminars to help people in all aspects of their life, not just spiritual. Saturday's presenter, who's in our congregation, just bailed. The topic is how to buy a home, and it's designed for young couples just starting out. About thirty people are signed up. Could you possibly fill in? I realize it's super short notice, but you know that stuff inside out—and you might pick up a couple of new clients."

She angled away from her laptop and gave the conversation her full attention. "Did Brad know you were going to ask me?"

"No. He doesn't get involved in the program other than approving the topics. The sessions are two hours, by the way. From one to three."

"Will he be there?"

"He sometimes stops in for a few minutes, but not always. It depends on his schedule for the day. Why?"

Because since he'd texted her that his evening with Stephanie had been a bust and his blind dating days were over, their next meeting could be awkward. And she'd prefer it not to be in front of a roomful of people.

"Just curious." A true answer, if not complete. And Laura did sound like she was in a bind. What could be the harm in helping her out? Once the presentation was over, she could make a fast exit. "Okay, kiddo. I'll be there."

"Thank you so much. You're a lifesaver."

After they said their goodbyes, Sam turned back to the seller's disclosure, a prickle of nerves skittering through her.

Not because of the presentation. She could do a talk like that in her sleep.

But what if Brad came? What if he was mad because his blind date had flopped? While his follow-up had been cordial, it was hard to get a clear read on people's mood in a text.

If luck was with her, though, he'd be a no-show for her presentation.

Unfortunately, however, Saturday wasn't her lucky day.

Not long after she launched into her presentation, Brad entered through the rear door of the meeting room and slipped into a seat in the back.

Her heart lurched, and she stumbled over a phrase, drawing a few raised eyebrows from the audience.

Sheesh.

This was crazy. She was a pro. A master at giving polished presentations.

She needed to refocus.

And the best way to do that was to ignore the distraction in the room.

Easier said than done, but after years in the business world she'd learned how to corral her nerves. And once she regained her stride, she made it through the presentation with no more missteps. At the end, she opened the floor to questions, handling them with her usual aplomb. Then she hung around to field individual questions from the attendees who descended on her.

Only when the group began to disperse did she risk a peek toward the back of the room.

Brad's chair was empty.

As a wave of disappointment swept over her, she shut down her laptop and blew out a breath.

She ought to be glad he'd taken off. Now she wouldn't have to—

The back door opened and he walked back in…sending her pulse off the scale yet again.

At least he was smiling as he strolled toward her. "Great presentation. I wish my sermons were that dynamic."

"Thanks." She took a deep breath. Now that they were alone, may as well address the elephant in the room. "Listen, I'm sorry your date with Stephanie fell flat. And I'm sorry if I was too pushy about setting it up. I understand why you'd be upset, and I—"

"Whoa." He frowned and held up his hand. "I'm not upset. Why would you think that?"

She wiped her palms down her skirt. "Well, your text was definitive about never doing that again, and I haven't heard from you since, so I assumed you were annoyed with me."

"Not at all." He blew out a breath and raked his fingers through his hair. "That's the problem with electronic communication. It doesn't always reflect nuances or emotion." He motioned to the empty rows of chairs. "Do you have to rush off, or can we sit for a minute?"

The coil of tension in her stomach unwound. "I can stay for a bit."

He followed her to the first row, sat, and angled toward her. "First, let's clear the air about my date. Stephanie is a nice woman, and we had a lot in common. But there wasn't any spark, for want of a better word. Don't ask me why, because on the surface it seemed like a solid match."

"Maybe you're just not ready to dive into dating again."

"No." His head shake was definitive. "A spark is either there or it's not. But I do appreciate your effort to liven up my lackluster social life."

"Hey, what are friends for? But after the succinct text I got from you, I was beginning to think our newly minted friendship was already history."

"I apologize if it came across as brusque. The week after that date was hectic, and for the past few days my father's been here visiting."

"Does he still live in southern Missouri? I've heard a lot about your hometown through the years from Laura."

"Yes. My mom died about six months ago, and Dad's having a tough time regrouping."

A pang of sympathy echoed in her heart. "I'm sorry for your loss. I'm sure that's been hard on both of you."

"On the whole family. I have my work, and my sister, Rebecca, has her restaurant in Ste. Genevieve, so we've kept busy, but for Dad—well, Mom was his north star. After she died, he lost interest in everything. Even his gardens, which were always his pride and joy. He hasn't even touched them this year."

She nodded. "It's hard when people you love are hurting. Harder still if you're physically in a different place. The importance of presence is underrated."

"Yes, it is. But you'd think after losing Rachel, not to mention all my years as a minister, I'd be able to find a way to break through with Dad. Instead, I'm batting zero. So is Rebecca. She gets down there as often as she can, but since she opened the restaurant she hardly has a minute to call her own."

"Have you made any headway with him during his visit here?"

"No. His spirits are still in a major slump. I wish I could find something that would perk him up." He squinted at her. Cocked his head. "Or some*one*." He took a deep breath. "I don't suppose there's any chance you're free tonight and would consider having dinner with us, would you? You're always so animated and out-going and fun to be with. If you can't brighten Dad's day, no one can."

He thought she was fun to be with?

Best news she'd had in months.

But foisting a stranger on a man who was grieving could backfire.

As she crossed her legs, Brad's gaze flicked to them. "How do you think your dad would feel about being forced to eat with a stranger, especially if he's feeling down?"

He refocused on her face "I'll, uh, lay the groundwork. I can tell him I wanted to thank you for filling in for us today. That wouldn't be a lie. But I also don't want to put you on the spot. I'm sure you already have plans. And even if you don't, there are more exciting things you could do than have dinner with us—like clean out your closets or vacuum the furniture." He grinned as he gave her an out…but his eyes were still hopeful.

"As a matter of fact, I don't have plans for tonight. I'd love to join you."

"Are you sure?" He scrutinized her.

"Yes. Just tell me when and where."

"Why don't we pick you up at six?"

"I could meet you at the restaurant if that's easier. I mean, this isn't a date or anything."

"True. Not too many guys would bring their fathers along on

a date. I do remember that much about the rules of the game." He hitched up one side of his mouth, then grew more serious. "But with all the bad stuff in the world today, I'd feel better seeing you home afterward. Call me old-fashioned."

She smiled as warmth bubbled up inside her. "I'd prefer to call you chivalrous. And I accept. Is casual attire okay?"

"Perfect. Why don't I walk you to your car before I turn off the lights and lock up?"

"No need. It's broad daylight, and I'm in a church parking lot. Go ahead and shut down here so you can get home to your dad. I'll see you at six."

"I'll bow to your logic."

Nevertheless, he walked her to the door, and as Sam continued to her car and drove toward her condo, she couldn't rein in the smile tugging at her lips.

She ought to be sorry Brad and Stephanie hadn't clicked, of course. And it was kind of surprising they hadn't. They'd seemed like such an excellent match.

Yet Brad seemed to prefer spending time with a red-haired real estate agent he'd called animated and outgoing and fun to be with.

Not that she should read too much into his comment, of course. Enjoying someone's company for a coffee date or symphony performance wasn't like contemplating a lifetime commitment. A man who'd admitted he was lonely no doubt found someone like her a novelty. A quick fix for a dull day.

But every now and then, a look stole into his eyes that suggested his interest was more than superficial.

Wouldn't it be nice if that was true?

Yet even if it was, there was no future for them.

Because she didn't deserve a man like Brad.

And she never would.

5

"I don't know why you had to invite a stranger to have dinner with us."

As Brad pulled up in front of Sam's condo and set the brake, he took a calming breath.

This was not shaping up to be a pleasant evening. His father had been grousing about their dinner arrangements for the past two hours.

"I told you, Dad." He kept his tone conversational. "She did the church a favor today by stepping in at the last minute to do a presentation for us. She's a nice woman. You'll like her."

"Hmph."

As his father folded his arms, Brad clenched his fingers around the wheel.

So much for this great idea.

Even worse?

Railroading Sam into an awkward situation might *de*rail their budding friendship.

If he could back out, he'd do it in a heartbeat.

But she pushed through the door of her condo, taking that option off the table.

He was stuck.

"There she is, Dad." He motioned toward her as he opened his door. "I'll be right back."

He left the car behind, lengthening his stride to meet her half-way down the walk.

"Hi." She smiled as he approached. "I saw you pull up from my window and thought I'd save you a few steps." She tipped her head. "What's wrong?"

"Honestly? I was just wondering if there was a gracious way to cancel."

Her lips flatlined, and some of the brightness faded from her eyes. "If you've changed your mind, I won't hold you to your invitation. I wouldn't want to embarrass you in front of your father."

What?

He furrowed his brow as he tried to make sense of her comment. "I'm not sure what you mean."

Her mouth twisted. "I toned down my makeup, and I chose my most modest attire, but this was the best I could do. I'm not exactly the demure type." She fiddled with the V neckline of the top she wore over skinny black pants.

A shock ricocheted through him as her meaning sank in.

The feisty, confident woman he was getting to know thought he was ashamed to be seen with her? That she was too flashy for a minister? That she somehow wasn't good enough to be his friend?

Pressure built in his throat, and he reached over. Touched her arm. "That isn't what I meant, Sam. I would never be embarrassed to be seen with you. I meant that my dad has been complaining nonstop since I told him I'd invited someone he doesn't know to eat with us. I'm afraid this could be very uncomfortable, and that you might resent me pushing you to join us."

She caught her lower lip between her teeth as she scrutinized him. "Seriously?"

"As God is my witness."

After a moment, the tension evaporated from her features and she smiled. "In that case, let's get this show on the road. I like a challenge. And I have a feeling our dinner will turn out fine."

"I like your optimism." He pivoted and crooked his arm. "Okay. Let's give this a go."

As she slipped her arm through his and they started back to the car, his father slid out of the passenger seat, posture stiff. As if he was bracing for an ordeal.

Brad forced up the corners of his lips as they approached. "Dad, this is Sam Reynolds. Sam, meet my father, Henry."

Sam extracted her arm from his, held out her hand, and offered his dad one of her megawatt smiles. "It's nice to meet you, Mr. Matthews. Thanks for letting me join you tonight. It's not often that a woman gets a chance to go out with *two* handsome men."

His father's expression remained stoic as he took her hand and parroted back the nice-to-meet-you line. "I'll sit in the back."

Before anyone could protest, he opened the rear door and slid in, closing it behind him.

Brad gave Sam an I-told-you-so eye-roll as she moved toward the front passenger seat, but she just winked and grinned.

His father was quiet during the drive to the restaurant, answering Sam's questions politely but in as few words as possible. Once seated at their table, she tried again to draw him out as they perused the menu, with little success.

But she was making a yeoman effort, God bless her.

After they ordered, she linked her fingers on the table and focused on his dad. "Brad tells me you're a gardener."

"Used to be." He fiddled with his napkin.

"What do you grow?"

"Roses and perennials."

"What's your favorite rose variety?"

"Tea roses."

"Same here. Do you have any Double Delights?"

His eyebrows rose as he made eye contact with her. "A couple."

"That's the best-smelling rose I've ever grown."

His father tilted his head. "You grow roses?"

"Yes. Perennials too. I have a little garden around the edge of my patio at the back of my condo. But I have a feeling yours is a lot bigger."

"It's a fair size, I guess. Thirty-two tea roses, and a couple of nice-sized perennial beds."

"Wow. I only have eight roses and a few perennials. I wish I had room for more. How long have you been at this, Mr. Matthews?"

"All my life. And you can call me Henry." He helped himself to a roll from the basket. A positive sign for a man who had to be coaxed to eat these days. "I've always liked flowers. Lots of people don't bother with roses, though. They claim they're too much trouble."

"That's crazy." Sam waved that notion aside. "Spray them once a week, feed them once a month, cover the roots for the winter—how hard is that?"

"Exactly." His dad's eyes lit up. "They're no trouble at all, considering they bloom all summer. What kind of spray do you use?"

As Sam and his father launched into a lively discussion about the merits of various fungicides for black spot, Brad sat back and watched.

Who would ever have guessed that Sam, with her sophisticated clothes and polished nails, was a gardener?

Apparently, with Laura's best friend it was smart to expect the unexpected—and to never underestimate her.

Like tonight.

Despite her outgoing nature and optimism, he'd have laid odds that this dinner would be a disaster.

Instead, she'd done what no else had been able to—drawn his father into an animated conversation and put a sparkle back in his eyes. She even got him to laugh.

Brad shook his head.

As far as he was concerned, that was a miracle.

By the time they arrived back at her condo after an extended meal, Sam and his father were chatting as if they'd known each other for years.

"You aren't going to neglect those poor roses anymore, are you, Henry?" Sam angled around in her seat as Brad stopped in front of her condo.

"Nope. I plan to tackle 'em first thing when I get home. And you won't forget to send me some of those perennial hollyhock seeds, will you? They sound mighty pretty."

"I promise to put them in the mail next week. " Sam held out her hand, and his dad gave it a vigorous shake.

"It's been a pleasure. And you're welcome any time to come see my gardens after I get them back in shape. Maybe Brad'll bring you down some weekend."

Sam sent a sidelong look toward the driver's seat. "He's a busy man, Henry. But I'll be sure to stop by if I ever find myself in your neighborhood. In the meantime, try that spray I told you about. It works wonders in this Missouri humidity. I haven't had a touch of black spot since I started using it."

"I sure will. And thanks for having dinner with us, Sam. It was fun."

"It was my pleasure."

"I'll walk Sam to her condo, Dad." Brad opened his door.

"No hurry. You two take your time."

Before he could circle the hood, Sam was already out of the car. "Why don't we say goodbye here?" She tipped her head toward the back seat. "I hate to keep your dad waiting."

"No way. I'd never hear the end of it if I didn't walk a lady to her door."

She shook her head. "You're a rare breed, Brad Matthews. At least in my world."

He fell in beside her as they strolled toward her condo. "The men in your acquaintance don't have good manners?"

"Maybe they would with a lady. I don't think they consider me in those terms." She gave him a flippant smile as she scanned her access card for the lobby...but a shadow of hurt hovered at the edges.

He pushed the door open and followed her in. "I hope you won't think I'm being too opinionated, but if the men you hang around with don't treat you like a lady, they aren't worth your time."

She shrugged. "It's the image I've cultivated. And you reap what you sow—as the Good Book says. I'm sure you could quote me chapter and verse on reference."

"Galatians 6:7."

"See?"

He continued to follow her, trying without success to fit together pieces that didn't dovetail. "I'm struggling with a disconnect, Sam. You've told me your party girl reputation is exaggerated. Yet you continue to foster it. I'm trying to connect the dots and—

"Sam? Is that you?" An older woman in the condo next to Sam's opened her door halfway and peered down the hall.

"Hello, Mrs. Johnson. Yes, it is." Sam continued toward her, stopping a few feet away.

"I thought I spotted you out my window, but I've misplaced my glasses again. I'm sorry to bother you, dear, especially since you have a gentleman friend with you, but did you have a chance to pick up those items for me?"

"Yes, I did. I'll bring them over in a few minutes."

"Thank you so much. You go ahead and say goodnight to your young man first." The woman aimed a smile his direction and shut the door.

When Sam looked at him, there was a faint hint of pink on her cheeks. "Sorry about that 'your young man' business. And I'm afraid your father has the wrong impression about our relationship too."

She wasn't going to respond to his disconnect comment.

And for now, it might be best to let it go.

But at some point he intended to circle back to that unsolved puzzle.

"No worries. People often jump to conclusions based on circumstantial evidence."

"Too true." She continued to her door.

"So what was the exchange with your neighbor all about?"

"It's kind of a sad story." Sam fitted the key in her lock and turned to him, brow puckered. "She's eighty-five, and her kids want to put her in an assisted living facility. But she's doing her best to hang on to her independence. As far as I can see, she's perfectly able to look after herself with a bit of help. Like someone to do her grocery shopping every week and pick up a prescription now and then."

"And that someone is you?"

She lifted one shoulder. "Why not? I'm out and about all the time. Adding an errand here or there is no big deal to me, but it makes a big difference to her."

Yet another appealing facet of this woman who had far more depth and dimension than a casual observer might notice. Not to mention a caring heart.

"That's still a very thoughtful thing to do. Many people wouldn't bother."

The corners of her mouth flexed. "Who knows, maybe someone will do the same for me when I'm old and alone." Despite her light tone there was sadness deep in her eyes as she angled away and twisted the key in the lock.

Only after she turned back to him did he speak. "What makes you think you'll be alone?"

She swallowed. "Let's just call it intuition." She moistened her lips. "You should go. Your dad is waiting"

"He said we should take our time."

"I know, but there's no reason to leave him in the car by himself any longer than necessary."

Yes, there was.

He had questions that needed answers.

But how could he broach them without scaring her off?

Maybe he could lead into them gradually.

"I appreciate what you did for him tonight."

"It was no effort. He's a nice man."

"Where did you learn so much about flowers?"

Her mouth flexed. "I've always enjoyed gardening."

"You never mentioned that before."

"It just never came up."

He propped a shoulder against the wall and folded his arms.

"It seems I learn something new about you every time we're together. I guess that's what happens in a developing friendship."

"I guess so." Her response came out choppy as she looked up at him with her vivid green eyes.

A tingle zipped through him, and all at once friendship was the last thing on his mind.

His gaze dropped to her lips as his pulse picked up.

Kissing Sam wasn't on the agenda for this evening's dinner. But a taste of her lips would be far sweeter than the cheesecake he'd enjoyed for dessert.

Bad idea, Matthews.

Electricity aside, the two of them were too different for anything to come of a romance. And he wasn't in the market for a relationship that didn't have serious potential.

He needed to get out of here before he made a mistake they could both come to regret.

"Well...I should be going." He pushed off from the wall and took a step back. "Let me know if you find a house that might work for me."

"I will." Something that looked a lot like longing flared in her eyes, so potent it might have undermined his resolve to beat a hasty retreat if she hadn't jerked around, fumbled with the doorknob, and slipped into her condo with a breathless thank-you for dinner.

When the lock clicked into place on the other side of the door, Brad sucked in a lungful of air.

That had been close.

Too close.

Nice as Sam was, the ground rule for them had been friendship from the beginning.

Yet if he'd been reading her correctly just now, she was getting other ideas—as was he.

That didn't mean it would be smart to pursue them, however. And he needed to keep that in mind going forward.

Three minutes later, he returned to the car to find his father in the front passenger seat—and much more upbeat than *he* was.

"Sam sure is a nice girl." His dad focused on him as he slid behind the wheel.

Girl?

Most women these days wouldn't appreciate that term, but Brad refrained from pointing that out to his father as he put the car in gear and exited the parking spot. "Yes, she is."

"Have you known her long?"

"Since Laura's wedding. She was the maid of honor."

"Let's see, that's been…what? Two months ago?"

"About that."

"And you've been seeing her ever since?"

At the speculative tone in his father's voice, Brad sent him a warning look. "Don't get any ideas, Dad."

"Why not? She's the first woman you've noticed in years, as far as I know. And she's worth noticing. Couldn't find anyone peppier or smarter or more fun to be around. Plus, she's a looker. What more could a man want?"

"Nothing—if a man was in the market for romance. I'm not. Sam and I are just friends."

His father guffawed.

As Brad flipped on the turn signal, he glanced over at him. "What's that supposed to mean?"

"Son, I may be old, but my eyesight is fine. I watched you tonight, and when you look at Sam I don't see friendship in your eyes."

Uh-oh.

If his dad was picking up the interest he was trying to keep in check, was Sam tuned into it too? Had she also felt the sizzle of attraction that made the air crackle whenever they were together?

"Well?" Dad angled toward him.

"Well what?"

"What are you going to do about it?"

This was not a discussion he wanted to have.

"Nothing. You're jumping to too many conclusions way too soon."

"Baloney." He waved that off. "I knew your mother was the one for me two weeks after we met. Took her a little bit longer, but we got married six months later. So two months isn't too soon to get interested. And in case you haven't noticed, the interest is mutual."

Apparently he hadn't misread the longing in Sam's eyes before she'd gone into her condo.

But that didn't change anything.

"I'm not ready for a serious relationship, Dad."

A few beats ticked by, and when his father spoke again his voice was gentle. "It's been six years, son, and you're still a young man. It's not too late to have that family you always wanted. Rachel was a wonderful woman, but she's gone and she wouldn't want you to be alone. You know that."

Yeah, he did.

"I hear what you're saying." He tightened his grip on the wheel. Swallowed. "But it's hard to let go."

His dad's protracted sigh spoke louder than words, as did the sudden melancholy in his voice. "That's for sure."

Brad glanced over at him. Some of the life had left his eyes, dampening the spark Sam had fanned back to life.

Maybe if he refocused Dad on her, he could perk him back up.

"I take it you like Sam."

"What's not to like? She's got spirit. And did you see how her eyes shine when she talks about gardening? I can't believe somebody hasn't grabbed her up by now."

"As a matter of fact, she was married once. Years ago."

"Is that right? What happened?"

He hesitated—but perhaps sharing the basics would be okay. Sam had been upfront about her failed marriage. "She was only eighteen. He was a musician. He walked out on her after a few months."

His dad gave a snort of disgust. "Guy must have been a real loser to leave someone like Sam behind. She still in touch with him?"

"No. He died years ago."

"Hmm." A few seconds passed as the distant wail of a siren pierced the night air. "An experience like that could make a body gun-shy of taking the plunge again. But I expect the right man could convince her to give marriage another go."

"Maybe." He passed a slower-moving car. "But even if I was ready to think about finding someone new, Sam and I are too different to get seriously involved."

"Doesn't seem that way to me. Far as I can tell, you two get along fine. Maybe you have a lot more in common than you think."

He let that pass.

And for the remainder of the drive, he switched the conversation to Rebecca and the success she was enjoying with her restaurant.

Yet as he prepared for bed later, the exchange with his father replayed through his mind.

Interesting that Dad had picked up on the sparks between him and Sam.

Because much as he might want to deny they existed, he'd only be fooling himself. And they intensified with every encounter as new aspects of her personality and character kept surfacing.

Like her ability to connect with a man who was grieving and put a glint of life back in his eyes. Or her kindness toward her older neighbor. Or the volunteer work she did on Tuesday nights. She'd played the latter low-key and offered no details, but that seemed to be how Sam operated. She did good things but never called attention to them.

Whether she attended church or not, she was living the principles he preached every week from the pulpit.

He recapped his toothpaste. Wandered back into the bedroom.

Maybe his dad was right. Maybe he and Sam *did* have more in common than he'd thought. Dating a nonchurchgoing woman wasn't the best move for a minister, but Sam had said she was a believer. So maybe that hurdle could be overcome. With exposure to church as it was meant to be, she might consider restarting her lapsed faith practices.

That wasn't out of the realm of possibility.

And considering the magnetism between them, their compatibility on other levels also seemed worth exploring.

Slowly, and with great caution, of course.

He flipped on the bedside lamp. Sat on the edge of the mattress.

A safe place to start might be the annual church picnic. A simple, unpretentious event with no hint of romance that would allow him to introduce her to his church family while continuing to get to know her better.

He swung his legs into bed. Pulled up the sheet. Flipped off the light.

No need to make any rash decisions. He'd sleep on that idea. Ponder it for a few days. And then, if he could work up the courage to start down a path that could be rife with unknowns, he'd give her a call and extend the invitation.

* * *

Brad was calling her.

As his name flashed on her cell, Sam's pulse stumbled.

No surprise there, since it had been doing the same thing whenever that moment in the hallway outside her condo four days ago replayed through her mind. The moment she could have sworn he'd had kissing on his mind. The moment when an overpowering longing had swept over her and *she'd* almost initiated a kiss.

She closed her eyes. Took a deep breath.

Thank goodness she'd had the fortitude to turn away and escape into her condo. Otherwise, she could have ruined their friendship.

And that's all it was to Brad. All it would ever be, even if loneliness might awaken a fleeting yearning when he was in her presence.

As for her, friendship was all it *could* ever be, no matter how much she wished it might be more. No matter what she thought she'd seen in his eyes.

Quashing an uncharacteristic wave of self-pity, she checked on the clients doing a walk-through of the house they were interested in and tucked herself into a quiet corner of the dining room. "Morning, Brad." She put as much cheer into her voice as she could muster into her greeting.

"Good morning. Do you have a minute?"

"Yes. I'm waiting for a couple to finish viewing a house."

"I won't keep you long. Thanks again for going to dinner with me and my dad the other night. You really perked him up. He went home early because he was anxious to get his gardens back in shape."

She smiled. "That's great news. Tell him I mailed those hollyhock seeds to him yesterday, by the way."

"I will. But I could have saved you the postage. I'm going down there over Memorial Day weekend with Rebecca. Our plan was to try to cheer him up, but thanks to a certain redhead that goal has already been accomplished. I'd cancel except that Rebecca needs a vacation, and if I don't go I doubt she will either."

"I'm sure your dad will enjoy having you both home."

"It will be nice for us too. I don't see either of them often enough anymore. But since you're in the middle of a showing, let me get to the main reason for my call. Our church picnic is the first Sunday in June, and I thought you might enjoy it. One of the couples in our congregation has a farm about forty-five minutes from St. Louis, and they let us use it every year. The picnic's nothing fancy, but it's always fun."

As Sam digested his invitation, she stared at a water stain on the hardwood flood that she'd have to point out to her clients.

Was Brad asking her out on a date? Or was this just a casual invite, one friend to another?

No clue.

She could ask, but what if he said it was a date?

That would be dicey.

Because if he showed a deeper interest in her beyond friendship, she'd have to stop seeing him. Immediately. Otherwise, she'd build up false expectations that could end up hurting him when she pulled back.

And the last thing she wanted to do was hurt Brad.

When the silence lengthened, he spoke again, a hint of amusement in his voice. "Just to clarify—this isn't a revival meeting in disguise. There will be no sermon and no hymn singing. It's purely social. But I can't promise to be super attentive while we're there. I tend to get pulled in a dozen directions at church events."

In other words, this wasn't a real date.

Perfect.

"No worries. I know how to take care of myself in social settings. And yes, I'd like to go."

A beat ticked by, as if he was surprised she'd accepted, but he recovered fast. "Great. I'll call you with details after I get back. And I hope you make a sale today."

She glanced at the couple huddled in the adjacent kitchen, talking in low tones. "I'm getting positive vibes."

"Fingers crossed."

"Thanks. Safe travels."

Once they severed the connection, Sam tucked her cell back into her purse and tried to tamp down the sudden uptick in her spirits.

This wasn't a date. Nor did she want it to be. But how could she not look forward to spending an afternoon in the company of a man who had all the stellar qualities that would make him a superlative catch for some lucky woman?

Even if that lucky woman wasn't her.

* * *

"So tell me about Sam." Rebecca licked her ice cream cone and angled sideways in her seat on the back porch of their childhood home.

Brad took a bite of his own ice cream.

His sister's question wasn't unexpected. Not after the speculative look she'd given him when they arrived earlier in the day and his father immediately asked about Sam.

"What do you mean?"

Rebecca rolled her eyes. "Give me a break, big brother. You know exactly what I mean. What's the scoop?"

"You're eating it." He nodded towards her cone.

"Ha ha. Spare me the bad puns. I hope you do better than that in your sermons. And don't try to change the subject. I want to know about Sam."

"She's my real estate agent."

"Oh." Her face fell for a moment, but then she squinted at him. "Why does Dad know her?"

"You know her too. You met her at Laura's wedding. She was the maid of honor."

"The redhead?"

"Yep."

"I remember her." She nodded. "We didn't get much of a chance to talk, but she seemed perky and upbeat."

"That would be Sam." He crunched into his cone.

Silence.

Rebecca huffed out a breath. "If that's all you're going to say, I'll have to give Dad the third degree."

Not a good idea. Dad might share whatever matchmaking ideas were percolating in his brain.

"What do you want to know?"

"Everything." She leaned forward and gave him her full attention.

"Everything is a tall order."

"Fine. We'll play twenty questions. Why does Dad seem to know her so well?"

"She had dinner with us when he was in town. In fact, she's responsible for that miracle." He motioned toward their father, who was weeding the perennial bed. "The two of them had a lively discussion about gardening, and the next thing I knew Sam was sending him seeds in the mail." The corners of his mouth edged up.

Rebecca studied him, a hint of incredulity in her eyes. "I think you're falling for this woman."

His lips flatlined. Yes, he liked Sam. And yes, he was attracted to her. But love was a distant speck on the horizon. "I wouldn't go that far. I only met her two months ago."

"It doesn't take long if it's the right person."

"And you know this how?"

Despite his teasing tone, Rebecca's hand paused for a nanosecond as she raised the ice cream cone to her mouth.

He winced.

If she hadn't put him on the defensive, he'd have thought before he spoke. Rebecca had always been sensitive about the lack of romance in her life.

"Becca...I'm sorry." He reached over and touched her shoulder.

She gave a stiff shrug. "It's okay. You're right. I'm no authority on the subject."

But why wasn't she?

The same question that had looped through his mind over the years echoed again. Since her childhood, she'd loved romantic stories. Had dreamed of having her own home someday and filling it with children.

But at some point she'd stopped mentioning all that. And as far as he knew, she rarely dated. Instead, she poured all her energy and passion into her business.

It didn't make sense.

He licked off a wayward drip from his cone and approached the subject with caution. "You could be. You have so much love to give. You should have a husband and a house full of kids to share it with. I'm guessing there's a reason you don't. Would you like to talk about it?"

Several seconds passed, the silence broken only by the chirp of the cicadas. When she at last turned to him with a smile that seemed forced, there was a slight sheen in her eyes. "Thanks for the offer, big brother. I know your listening skills are a huge asset in your ministry, but I'm fine. Please don't worry about me. I have a good life."

He could push—but Rebecca wouldn't talk unless she was in the mood to unburden her soul, and it was clear she wasn't tonight.

"I'm here if you ever want a sympathetic ear."

"I know. And I appreciate that. But we were talking about *your* love life, remember?" She crumbled her paper napkin in her fist. "Rachel was a wonderful woman, but maybe it's time to let her go. To find someone new to love, and to have that family you always wanted. You'd be a fabulous father."

"I have to admit I've been thinking along those lines lately."

"Because of Sam."

It was an assumption, not a question, and protesting too much would only solidify the conclusion she'd already come to. "There were a number of factors at play."

"Well, whatever the impetus, I'm happy for you." She tossed the bottom of her cone into the yard for the birds to fight over and waved a hand toward the garden. "Do you think we should drag Dad in before the mosquitoes finish him off?"

"Yes. I don't know how he can see in the dark, anyway."

The conversation took a different turn when it became a threesome, so it wasn't until much later that Brad had a chance to mull over his conversation with Rebecca.

Her instincts seemed spot-on. He and Sam could be heading in a serious direction. It wasn't love yet, but that could be coming down the road.

And more and more, he was open to that possibility.

He fingered the wedding ring that had never left his finger since he'd said I do.

One of these days, if he was serious about moving on, it would have to come off.

Perhaps sooner rather than later.

* * *

Sam eyed herself in the full-length mirror in her bedroom. Frowned.

Even though she'd run her attire past Laura, a wave of second thoughts swept over her.

Her khaki shorts were a modest length, and her sleeveless cotton blouse was far less revealing than the tank tops she favored for summer attire—but still. This was a church picnic. Maybe a skirt would have been more appropriate.

Except that would have been just as short as her shorts.

She sighed.

At least her sedate, tucked-in French braid and toned-down makeup should pass muster. Very respectable and—

Her doorbell chimed, and she took a deep breath.

Too late now to make any changes.

Wiping her palms down her shorts, she hurried to the door, twisted the knob—and tried to keep breathing as she took in

Brad's oh-so-nice-fitting jeans and a blue golf shirt that hugged his broad chest and called attention to his impressive biceps.

He hiked up an eyebrow, amusement sparking in his blue irises. "Do I pass?"

Warmth bloomed on her checks.

Dang.

So much for the skill she'd developed through the years to tame the blush that was the bane of most redheads.

"You look fine. I've just, uh, never seen you dressed that casual."

"Did you think I'd wear my clerical attire to a picnic?"

"Well, it *is* a church event. I thought you might have to keep up a certain image with your congregation."

He offered her a full-out grin. "They've seen me in civvies before. Unless I'm performing official duties, I try to dispense with anything that might be a barrier between me and the flock I'm supposed to tend."

Nice.

"That's also out of the realm of my experience. The ministers of my acquaintance were on the stuffy side. I always felt like they looked down on everyone from a higher plane."

Brad's lips contorted into a rueful twist. "That can turn a person off religion."

"You're looking at a case in point. But I'm revising my opinion, thanks to a certain minister who crossed my path."

"Then I consider our time together well spent."

As his words registered, her stomach bottomed out.

Was that why he was seeking her out? Why he wanted to befriend her? Because he saw her as a lost soul in need of saving?

His smile faded, and faint creases appeared on his brow. "What's wrong?"

She did her best to regroup. "Nothing."

A few beats passed as he studied her. "I don't think I'm buying that. Why don't you tell me what's on your mind?"

It was hard to keep up pretenses with this astute man.

And maybe she ought to be honest—then ask for honesty in return.

Taking a steadying breath, she waved him in. "Let's talk in here."

In silence he crossed the threshold. Turned to her.

She shut the door and swiveled around. "It occurred to me that your previous kindness and today's invitation may have more to do with your professional life than with friendship."

The furrows on his forehead deepened. "I'm not sure what you…" His voice trailed off as understanding dawned in his eyes. "You think I see you as some sort of evangelization project?"

"That did occur to me."

"Oh, man." He raked his fingers through his hair. "I guess this illustrates how out of practice I am at personal relationships."

"Listen, it's okay if—"

"Wait." He held up his hand. "Before we go any further, let me clear up any misperceptions. My primary interest in you has nothing to do with anything church-related. If your faith is bolstered by our interactions, I won't be unhappy. But that's not why I suggested we be friends. I'm seeing you because I like you."

Warmth bubbled up inside her. "For real?"

"Would a minister lie?"

"I hope not."

"Trust me, this one isn't. So unless you've changed your mind about being *my* friend, I hope we can continue seeing each other." The sincerity in his eyes was impossible to dispute.

"I haven't changed my mind."

He smiled. "In that case, shall we go to the picnic?"

"Yes." Spirits lifting, she picked up her purse off the foyer table.

During the drive to the farm, Brad told her about his trip home and she filled him in on the houses she'd looked at—and rejected—for him.

She was much more relaxed when they arrived...until they rounded the barn on the property and a momentary hush fell over the crowd as they came into sight.

Her step faltered.

She could schmooze and make small talk with the best of them, but this was a different kind of crowd. These were religious people. And many of them had probably known Rachel. Of course they'd be curious when their grieving minister brought a woman to a church event—and would assume there was more to his interest than friendship.

Had Brad thought about that?

She peeked over at him.

His eyes had narrowed almost imperceptibly as he gave the assemblage a sweep.

If he hadn't thought about it before, he was thinking about it now.

"I have a feeling I'm about to run the gauntlet." She lowered her voice, leaned closer to him, and tried for a teasing tone. No sense ignoring the obvious.

He looked down at her, his expression contrite. "Sorry. I guess I didn't stop to think how much interest your appearance would generate. You having second thoughts?"

"Too late for that. I've already been spotted. The damage is done."

"For the record, I don't consider it damage." He locked gazes with her for a moment, but before she could analyze the look in his eyes he crooked his elbow. "I'll make a circuit with you, do some introductions."

"Let's hope I pass muster." She slipped her arm through his.

"The only one you have to pass muster with is me, and that hurdle has already been cleared." His smile helped a tad to mitigate her sudden case of nerves.

They made the rounds of the small groups clustered near the barn, and though it was impossible to fault anyone's manners there was a subtle reserve in their greetings. As if they weren't yet sure whether to accept the intruder who had caught their minister's eye.

And really, how could she blame them? She was nothing like Brad's first wife, who had no doubt been beloved by his congregation.

Her spirits nosedived as they made their way toward two older women, who watched her and Brad approach with obvious curiosity.

After he finished the introductions, he turned to her. "Susie is our wonderful organist. Her playing always inspires me to sing." His lips twitched at Susie's pained expression.

"It's nice to meet you both." Sam shook their hands.

"Do you by any chance sing? We're always looking for good voices for the choir." Susie emphasized the word good, and Sam tried not to grin as Brad's comment from the wedding, about his lack of singing ability, echoed in her mind.

"I'm afraid I'm not much in the voice department. I'm more the I-like-to-sing-in-the-shower-but-you'd-need-earplugs-if-I-sang-in-public type."

"Well, I'm sure you have many other talents." Susie patted her arm. "And I think it's important to recognize our limitations.

For example, if you can't sing, it's better not to try. Don't you agree, Reverend?"

"Absolutely."

At Brad's solemn nod and the look of defeat on Susie's face, Sam conjured up a cough to disguise the chuckle she couldn't contain.

"We're on the hunt for lemonade, ladies, if you'll excuse us." Brad guided her away from the duo.

As soon as they were out of earshot, Sam grinned and gave him a shoulder nudge. "Susie's expression was priceless."

His mouth flexed. "Poor Susie. I ought to just shut up and make her life easier, but I really do like to sing. I've toned it down, though. So I don't think she minds quite as much."

"Sam! Brad!"

They turned in unison as Laura hurried toward them, waving two pieces of paper with identical numbers on them, a burlap sack draped over her arm. "Will you two help me out? I'm supposed to be organizing the games, but nobody wants to be the first to sign up. So I put you down for the three-legged race. Do you mind? I think once I have a couple of people on board, it will break the ice."

Sam gave the sack a doubtful once-over. "You know I'm not the athletic type."

"You don't have to be for this. It's a short race. Brad, talk her into it, will you, while I try to round up a few more people?" Laura handed Brad the sack and numbers and dashed off to recruit two more victims.

Sam looked up at him. "Now what?"

He hiked up his shoulders. "I'm game if you are."

Sam bit her lower lip.

Based on the little she knew about three-legged races, there was physical proximity involved. If Brad could make her heart vault into triple time with a mere look, how would her metabolism react if they were touching?

Still, it was just a game, and his whole congregation would be watching. There could be no safer context in which to get close to him, and this opportunity might never come again.

Maybe she ought to enjoy it.

"All right." She took one of the numbers. "But I wasn't kidding when I said I'm not athletic. If you want to win, I'd suggest you find another partner."

"I'll take my chances with you." Brad gave her a wink that sent a delicious tingle racing through her. "Turn around so I can pin your number on."

Sam pivoted, but when it was her turn to do the pinning her fingers seemed to have a mind of their own as they got up close and personal with his broad shoulders. While the day was warm, the air temperature had nothing to do with the sudden surge of heat that shot straight to her core.

"All done." She stepped back. His number was slightly crooked, but it was good enough.

He turned back to her and opened the bag. "Okay, step in with one leg."

In silence, she followed his instructions.

He straightened up and put his leg in beside hers. "Can you hold on to the excess burlap on your side?"

"Sure." She reached over to take it from him. Did a double take when the bare fourth finger of his left hand registered.

When had that happened?

But she had no time to dwell on that after he slipped his arm around her waist and pulled her close, until they were touching along the entire length of their bodies from ankle to shoulder.

81

Whoa.

"We should practice a little." Brad didn't sound the least affected by the physical contact. "I know there's a trick to this. You have to be in sync, establish a rhythm. You want to try it?"

She was still trying to comprehend the significance of his bare left hand and deal with the sensory overload of their proximity to manage more than a shaky nod.

"Let's give it a whirl on three."

As he counted down, she tried to refocus—a chore that turned out to be easier than expected when it quickly became apparent that staying upright demanded her full and undivided attention. In fact, at their lame attempts to find a gait that would accommodate their disparate heights, hormones gave way to hilarity and she found herself giggling like a teenager.

"Hey, you two, no fair." Laura paused as she passed by. "If you practice, you'll have an advantage."

"I don't think you have to worry about that." Brad grinned at her. "This isn't a game you can master in one easy lesson. I see a lesson in humility in our future."

His words proved prophetic. Because despite their strong start after the gun went off, when Sam lost her footing soon after and clutched at his arm to regain her balance, she thew *him* off balance. As they pitched forward, he pulled her against him and twisted, taking the brunt of the impact.

The next thing she knew, she was sprawled across his firm, lean body, his arms still around her, his heart thudding against her ear.

It felt like an embrace.

And probably *looked* like one.

Oh, geez.

As wonderful as it felt in his arms, and as much as she

wouldn't mind extending this interlude, they needed to get up before his congregation suffered a collective heart attack at their shocking position.

Taking a deep breath, she backed off, bracing her hands on either side of him. "Are you hurt?"

"No. Are you?"

She shook her head, her breath catching as he reached up to frame her face with his hands, his thumbs caressing her cheeks, the look in his eyes impossible to misinterpret.

And it had nothing to do with friendship.

It seemed the ground rules for their relationship were shifting.

Meaning she was going to have to make a hard call very soon, no matter what her heart might wish for.

6

"Hey, are you two okay?"

At Laura's concerned question, Sam rolled sideways, untangled her leg from the burlap sack, and scrambled to her feet. Brad stood as well and brushed himself off.

"I'm fine." She patted her French braid. "Just a little shaken up."

"Brad?" As Laura turned to him, Sam ventured a glance his direction.

He flexed his shoulder. "A few minor bruises, I think. Nothing serious."

Likely more than that, since he'd taken the brunt of the fall by twisting to cushion her impact as they nosedived.

"Thank goodness." Laura smoothed back some stray wisps that had escaped from her ponytail. "You guys have been good sports, but why don't you find a cool spot and be spectators for a while? I think you've had enough games for today."

"Yes. I think our games are over."

Sam swallowed as Brad directed that comment to her.

He wasn't talking about three-legged races.

Laura looked from one to the other, her expression speculative. "Well, chill out for a while. I'll talk to you both later." She tossed the comment over her shoulder as she made a hasty exit.

Now what?

A wave of panic washed over Sam.

This picnic was supposed to be a simple, friendly get-to-gether. Not the start of a romance.

She had to calm down. Get the left side of her brain into gear. And that wasn't going to happen with Brad standing inches away.

"I, uh, think I'll find the ladies' room. Will you excuse me for a couple of minutes?"

Before Brad could respond, she fled in the direction of the house, grabbing her purse from a folding chair en route.

Once in the privacy of one of the porta-potties the church had brought in for the event, Sam closed the door and fisted her hands.

Things were moving *way* too fast.

Or maybe she'd just ignored his signals.

Like the night he took her home after dinner with his father. She'd suspected then that he wanted to kiss her as much as she wanted to kiss him.

Apparently her intuition had been spot-on.

But she'd turned a blind eye to his interest.

Because she'd known that if his feelings ever deepened beyond friendship, she'd have to end their relationship. Brad was a fine man who deserved a woman equally fine, and she didn't qualify. Friendship was all she could offer him.

Sam gritted her teeth as her vision blurred.

She had no one but herself to blame for the mess she was in now. And she'd already waited too long to get out. It would only get worse if she let more time pass.

Straightening up, she tucked a few loose strands of hair back into her French braid in the claustrophobic confines of the portable stall.

She'd have to suck it up and get through the rest of this—

"…so surprised when they walked in."

"She's nothing like Rachel, is she?"

Sam stilled as two women passed by.

"That's putting it mildly." The first woman gave a humorless laugh. "Whatever do you think he saw…"

The voices faded away.

Decision confirmed.

She didn't belong here. Didn't fit the mold of a minister's friend, let alone *girl*friend.

So when they got back to her condo later, she'd find a way to tell him she couldn't see him anymore.

Even if it killed her.

In the meantime, the easiest way to survive the day was to make sure she and Brad were never alone.

* * *

He'd revealed too much about his feelings. That had to be why Sam was avoiding him.

Brad folded his arms and leaned against a convenient tree, watching from a distance while she laughed and chatted with members of his congregation, her demeanor lighthearted.

Her carefree manner was a façade, however. Her eyes were a tad too bright, her smile forced.

But why was she spooked by the amorous vibes she was picking up from him? It wasn't because they were one-sided. He may have been out of the dating game for a while, but he hadn't misread the longing in her eyes.

Yet she was running scared.

Or could she just be surprised? After all, he'd only recently come to grips with the fact himself that despite their differences, a relationship was worth exploring. Maybe she hadn't made that leap yet. She might still be hung up on apparent disparities between them.

Whatever the reason for her sudden skittishness, he wasn't going to have an opportunity to talk with her about it at the picnic.

He waved off a persistent fly as she disappeared into the barn with Laura and a few other women to retrieve the food.

At least he'd have her all to himself on the drive home. They could talk then.

"Reverend, could we intrude with some business for a minute?"

Brad swiveled toward the voice. Three members of the finance committee stood behind him.

Oh joy.

This must be about the HVAC bill that had just come in.

He called up a smile. "Of course."

Five minutes into a discussion that was much too nitty-gritty for a social event, a startled voice called out behind him.

"Watch out, everybody! A bee's nest just fell by the door."

Brad swiveled around as a murmur of alarm tittered through the crowd.

While the people near the barn scattered, Brad scanned the grounds for Sam. Laura and the other women who'd gone into the building with her were by the food table, but there was no sign of Sam. And she was easy to find in a crowd, with her striking red hair.

Was she still inside? And if so, had she heard the warning?

A sudden surge of adrenaline propelled him toward the barn door, just as she stepped out balancing a tray holding two cakes.

"Sam! Get back inside!" He waved his arm toward the barn and sprinted toward her.

She stopped. Peered his direction as she called out. "What?"

"Get back—"

Too late.

She gave a startled yelp. Jerked around. Cried out again as she dropped the tray and began swatting at the bees while she started to run.

Brad reached her in seconds, just as she stumbled. He steadied her and waved at the remaining bees, ignoring the sharp stings in his hand as he did his best to discourage the few remaining insects that seemed to prefer Sam to the icing and cake all over the ground.

By the time the last bee had been banished and he'd gotten her to safety, Sam's complexion was as white as the coconut frosting on the cakes she'd carried. There was a sting above her lip, another over her left eye, a third on her cheek, and all were already swelling.

The owner of the farm hurried over, her face a mask of concern. "Let's get her inside. Sandy's here and she can help."

Thank heaven the physician's schedule had allowed her to attend today's picnic.

"I sent John for my bag in the car." Sandy stepped forward, scrutinizing Sam. "Are you allergic to bee stings?"

Sam shook her head, the movement jerky and punctuated by soft moans and erratic respiration.

Sandy gave her a quick but thorough once-over. "Brad, could you carry her inside? She has multiple stings on her ankle, and she seems too shaky to walk."

Without a word, he put one arm around her shoulders, the other under her knees, and lifted her, cradling her in his arms. As she whimpered softly against his chest and tremors coursed through her, his gut clenched.

The owner led them to the guest room, and Brad set Sam on the bed.

"She may need to undress so I can assess the damage." When he didn't move, Sandy motioned to the door. "You'd better wait outside."

Right.

With a nod, he moved toward the door.

Laura slipped in as he exited. "I'll stay with her until you can come back in."

"Thanks."

For the next ten minutes he paced, trying to rein in his impatience.

Just when he was about to knock on the door and demand an update, Laura came out.

"Well?" He strode over to her.

"She's got about a dozen stings, enough to cause major discomfort but not enough to be dangerous."

Brad expelled a long breath and wiped a hand down his face. "Thank God."

"It looks like Sam wasn't the only victim." Laura tapped the back of his hand.

He glanced down. Two welts marred his skin, though the throbbing only now registered. But his pain was mild compared to what Sam must be experiencing. "I'm fine. Would you and Nick try to keep the party going? I know Sam would feel terrible if this incident disrupted the picnic any more than it already has. I'd do it myself, but I'd rather stick close to her."

"No problem. Sandy will let you know when you can go in."

As Laura exited, Brad took up a position outside the door.

Another ten interminable minutes passed before the physician appeared.

Sandy smiled. "Relax, Brad. She's okay. Uncomfortable, but okay."

"Can I take her home now?"

"Yes. I've already told her what she needs to do, but I'm not sure she took it all in. Are you planning to stay with her for a while?"

"Yes."

"Then let me repeat the instructions for you. An over-the-counter painkiller is fine, and this will help if the stings start to itch. Linda had it on hand." She passed over a bottle of calamine lotion. "I'd advise an ice pack for the swelling on her ankle. She has multiple stings in very close proximity, which is going to make walking difficult for a couple of days. After that, the swelling and redness will dissipate. In a week she'll hardly even know this happened. If she shows any kind of allergic reaction, like difficulty breathing or nausea, get her to an ER. But I don't expect that to happen."

"Got it." Sort of. Everything she'd said had registered on a peripheral level. All he wanted to do was see Sam. "Can I go in now?"

"Yes. She's decent. I'm going to rejoin the picnic."

Brad waited until she disappeared down the hall, then took a steadying breath before he turned the knob and walked inside.

Sam was sitting on the edge of the bed, an ice pack in hand, the brackets around her mouth and her pallor silent evidence of her pain.

She gave him a wan smile as he crossed the room. "I guess I look a mess, huh?"

Yeah, she did.

The welts near her upper lip, above her eye, and on her cheek were an angry red, but her right hand and left ankle had taken the brunt of the attack. Two of her fingers were swollen, and her ankle was puffy and covered with crimson welts.

His voice was hoarse when he responded. "You look fine to me. I'm just glad it wasn't worse. I'm so sorry this happened. We've never had an injury at any of these picnics."

"It's not your fault. Maybe I'm a magnet for bad luck." She tried to smile, but winced instead as her skin stretched. "Listen, I know this is a big event for your church, and everyone expects you to stay for the duration. I can rest here until you're ready to leave."

Was she serious?

"They can survive without me. I'm taking you home. Now."

Her eyes widened. "But I don't want to ruin your day."

"This isn't open for discussion. Can you make it to the car, or do you want me to carry you?"

She gave a soft snort. "If you keep lugging me around, the next thing we'll be dealing with is a back injury. I appreciate the offer, but I think I can manage if you help me up."

Being too bossy with an independent woman like Sam could backfire, so in silence he extended his hand.

She took it and he eased her to her feet, stomach clenching at her sharp intake of breath. "Sam, I—"

"I'll be fine, Brad." Her words were choppy. "Just…give me a minute." He waited while she dipped her head. Took several deep breaths. "I'm ready."

"We'll go out the back. It's closest to the parking area and we can avoid the crowd." He took her arm. "Lean on me if you need to favor your ankle."

She didn't respond, but she *did* lean on him. Another indication of how much she was hurting. Because Sam wasn't a leaner.

And when they reached the car and she eased herself into the front seat, her irises were shimmering.

Best plan? Get her home as fast as possible.

She didn't speak at all during the drive back into the city. Just tucked herself into the corner of his car and closed her eyes.

Fine by him.

He needed a little time to regroup—and come to grips with the fierce surge of protectiveness that had swept over him when the bees had descended on her.

If he'd had any doubts about how strong his feelings were for her, that had put them to rest. The thought of anyone—or anything—hurting Sam squeezed his heart in a vise.

He glanced over at her, the strong, sassy woman who suddenly seemed so fragile and defenseless and in need of nurturing.

And he wanted to provide that nurturing.

So as soon as she was feeling more like herself, he intended to find out why she was so wary about the idea of getting involved with him. And then he intended to put her concerns to rest.

Because their days of being just friends were over.

* * *

"Sam? You're home."

At the gentle touch on her shoulder, she opened her eyes to find Brad leaning toward her from the driver's seat, worry etched into his features.

"Okay."

But it wasn't. Pain was radiating through her ankle, and the prospect of walking to her door was as intimidating as the thought of taking the Missouri Real Estate Licensing Exam had been. Nevertheless, she couldn't stay in the car for the rest of the day.

"All right. Let's do this." She fumbled for the door handle.

"Stay put until I come around." Brad angled toward his door and slid from behind the wheel.

She didn't argue. The longer she could put off the looming walk, the better.

Unfortunately, he pulled her door open far too soon and leaned down. "How do you feel?"

Like she'd been attacked by a horde of kamikaze bees—but she toned that back.

"The stinging isn't quite as bad."

His forehead puckered "I think I can read between the lines on that answer. The offer of a lift—literally—is still open."

She managed a shaky smile. "Thanks. But what would the neighbors say?"

"I have a feeling Mrs. Johnson would approve. After all, she thinks I'm your young man." His lips quirked. "Come to think of it, maybe she needs her vision checked. *Young* is hardly an accurate description for me."

"It is when you're eighty-five."

"I'll concede that point. Ready?"

No.

But what choice did she have?

"Yes. And I apologize again about today."

"Not necessary. We'll have other picnics."

No, they wouldn't.

But this wasn't the time to share that news.

"If you could hold the ice pack and let me lean on you when I get out, I should be good."

Somehow, with an assist from him, she got to her feet. After he closed the door, he slipped his arm around her waist for the trek up the walkway.

As they entered, crossed the lobby, and trekked to her front door, a bead of sweat trickled down her temple.

But she was almost home. And once inside, she was heading straight for bed.

When she fumbled the key in the lock, Brad reached over, tugged it from her shaky fingers, and took care of the task. Once the lock clicked, he twisted the knob and pushed the door open.

She angled toward him. "I guess it's too late for you to go back to the picnic, isn't it?"

"The picnic is the last thing on my mind." He weighed the ice pack in his hand. "This needs a refill. I'd like to know you're settled in for the night before I leave."

He wanted to come in?

"You don't have to do that. I've ruined your day enough already."

"That's not true. I'll admit it didn't turn out exactly like I'd hoped, but ending it here with you will at least finish it off on a pleasant note."

How could she not invite him in after a comment like that?

"You're welcome to stay as long as you like, but I can't promise to be much company. Sleep is high on my agenda."

"I won't keep you up. I promise." He pushed the door open and led her over to the couch. "I'll refill the ice pack."

He disappeared toward the kitchen, but returned a couple of minutes later, easing onto the couch beside her and handing over the ice pack. "You should put this on your ankle. Doctor's orders." He bent down, slipped off her shoe, and lifted her leg to the coffee table. "I'll let you position it, though. The cold may not feel great at first, and I don't want to hurt you."

At his tender touch and tone, pressure built in Sam's throat. No man had ever treated her with such care and respect.

Before she could stop it, a tear slipped past her lower lashes and trailed down her cheek.

She leaned forward, averting her face as she positioned the ice pack, but she couldn't seem to stop the sudden waterworks.

Of course Brad noticed.

"I'm sorry you're hurting so much." He took her uninjured hand, his clasp solid and comforting.

She *was* hurting—but the bee stings weren't the reason for her tears. Her hurt went much deeper than that.

However, it was safer to let him think her tears were due to her injuries.

"Sorry. I-I never cry."

"You deserve a cry, after the day you've had."

Maybe.

But crying never solved anything or made a hurt go away.

After a minute or two, she managed to get the tears under control. And as soon as she could muster the strength, she gently retracted her fingers. "Thanks for the loan of your hand."

"Anytime." There was no misreading the serious intent in his eyes. Yet after a moment, he motioned toward her kitchen. "I'm not much of a cook, but if you have any microwave food in the freezer I'd be happy to heat it up for you. You missed dinner."

"So did you. Why don't you make something for yourself? I'm well stocked with quick-to-fix meals."

"Will you eat if I do?"

Much as she'd like to accommodate him, she needed to lie down. Desperately.

"To tell you the truth, I just want to go to bed."

"Then that's what you should do." He stood, then drew her to her feet. "Let's get you to the bedroom."

At any other time that comment would have set her heart aflutter with all sorts of romantic fantasies. But with the stings beginning to throb with renewed intensity, all she could think about was the oblivion of sleep that would bring relief from her misery.

Brad slipped his arm around her waist as she limped toward the bedroom. Once they reached the bed, he eased her onto the edge, then scrutinized her face. "If you'll tell me where to find your aspirin, I'll get them and some water. I'll also bring in the lotion Linda sent."

After she complied and he left to retrieve everything, she reached around and tried without success to unbraid her hair, thanks to the two swollen fingers that rendered her right hand almost useless.

Huffing out a breath, she continued to struggle until Brad returned and deposited the items he'd collected on the nightstand. "What's wrong?"

"I should be able to unbraid my hair myself, but my fingers aren't cooperating. And If I don't do it before I go to sleep it will be too tangled to get a comb through tomorrow."

A few beats of silence ticked by, and she glanced up to find him frowning.

Oh.

Maybe he thought she was angling for a hand with her hair. And for a minister—even one who had romantic inclinations—touching a woman's hair might push the boundaries of propriety.

But man, it would be wonderful to feel his hands in her hair. Just once.

So instead of giving him an out, she dipped her head and continued to work on her braid.

Maybe guilt would compel him to offer a hand—and create a memory she could tuck in her heart and pull out in the future whenever loneliness overwhelmed her.

* * *

He ought to offer to help Sam with her hair. After all, if he hadn't invited her to the picnic she wouldn't be covered in painful, incapacitating stings.

But a major red alert was beeping in his mind.

As she fumbled with the braid, however, he sucked it up and stepped in. "Why don't you let me do that?"

Her fingers stilled. "If you wouldn't mind, I'd appreciate it." She angled sideways on the bed.

Lowering himself beside her, he took a deep breath and eyed the elaborate do. Or at least it looked elaborate to him compared to the short, simple cut Rachel had favored. "Um…you'll have to tell me where to start."

"There are bobby pins up and down the sides of the braid. I think I managed to get one partly out at the bottom." Sam bent her head, exposing an expanse of creamy skin at her nape.

He flexed his fingers and tried not to fixate on the wispy strands of soft-looking hair that had escaped and lay on her neck.

Doing this without getting all hot and bothered was going to be a challenge.

He scanned her hair and spotted the pin in question. "I see it." He reached up and tugged it out. "Let me see if I can find the rest."

Pulse accelerating, he probed until he found all the elusive pins, pulling them out one by one with unsteady fingers until the braid hung free. And unless he was imagining it, Sam's respiration was as uneven as his when he finished.

"I think that's it." He set the last pin on the bed beside him and exhaled.

"Thanks." She reached around with her good hand and attempted to loosen the braid, but her shaky fingers fumbled the job.

He clenched his teeth.

Since he'd started this job, he may as well finish it.

"Let me do that for you."

She hesitated, but then slowly retracted her hand.

A muscle in his jaw twitched as he began to methodically unbraid her hair, trying as hard as he could to keep his imagination and hormones in check.

It was a losing battle.

When at last her hair was loose, he reached for the brush on her nightstand. She could probably manage that herself, but he wasn't ready for this to end. "I'll get some of the tangles out for you."

She didn't protest.

As he gently ran the brush though her sleek hair, nerve endings he didn't even know existed sprang to life in his fingertips.

Sweet mercy.

He'd better hurry up and finish before he did something she might not be ready for and shot himself in the—

The brush dislodged a small object from Sam's hair, and he paused as it fell onto the bed beside her.

She glanced at it, and with a sudden shriek shot to her feet and backed away, staring at it in horror.

It was a harmless, dead bee.

But Sam had reacted as if another swarm was after her.

Following his instincts, he stood and pulled her into his arms. "Hey, it's okay. The bee's dead."

The rigid lines of her body went limp, and she sagged against him. "I think I'm go-going to have a bee phobia f-for life."

"Understandable, after what happened today." He stroked her back, and she nestled against him as she battled another case of the shakes. "Take a few deep breaths." Advice he'd be wise to follow as well.

When her trembling at last subsided, he forced himself to ease away and guide her to the bed. Then he handed her the water and pain pills.

"Thanks." She downed the tablets. "Sorry I'm such a mess."

"No apologies necessary. I'd suggest you put on the calamine lotion, apply the ice bag, and rest." She could probably use some help with the lotion, but his self-control was already stretched to the breaking point.

"I will. Thank you for everything."

"No problem." He slid his fingers into his pockets. He wasn't leaving until he confirmed she was sleeping comfortably, but if he told her he intended to hang around until then she'd protest. He'd have to try a different departure delay tactic. "While you drift off, do you mind if I nuke some food from your freezer? I'm getting hungry."

"Of course not. Help yourself."

"I'll let myself out when I'm done. Call me later if you need anything. No matter how late it is."

"I'm not going to disturb your sleep."

"I won't sleep at all if you don't promise."

She cocked her head. "You can be stubborn."

"Determined."

"Semantics." But after a moment, she capitulated with a slight twitch of lips. "You win. But I'll be fine."

"I hope so, but I'll be available if you're not. If I don't hear from you, I'll call you tomorrow."

"Okay. Go have some dinner." She waved him toward the door.

He took the cue.

And once he ate a fettuccini dinner, cleaned up his dishes, and took a quick peek at her small but well-tended garden, he was ready to call it a night. His shoulder was aching, his own stings were throbbing, and exhaustion was settling over him like a coat of chain mail.

He tiptoed down the hallway, pausing to peek in the door of Sam's bare-bones, utilitarian bedroom. Not the kind of space he'd expected, based on the artsy, designer decor in the rest of the condo. It was almost as if she didn't care about this room because no one ever saw it except her.

Something she'd more or less implied in previous conversations, but a definite disconnect with the image he'd formed of her.

An image that had been disintegrating bit by bit since they'd met.

She appeared to be sleeping quietly, her breathing even, no signs of restlessness that could indicate pain, her glorious hair splayed across the pillow.

His heart skipped a beat, and he fisted his hands.

It was time for him to go. Even if he didn't want to.

In truth, if he had his druthers, he'd rack out on the couch. Stay within calling distance.

But ministers didn't spend a night in a woman's home. No matter how innocent or charitable the motivation, it stretched the bonds of propriety.

Fighting the temptation to ignore decorum, he retraced his steps down the hall toward the foyer, set the lock, and pulled the door shut behind him.

Hopefully, Sam would sleep through the night.

But he had a feeling *he* wasn't going to be so lucky.

7

Someone was calling her in the middle of the night?

Fighting off a major case of grogginess, Sam forced her eyelids open as her phone trilled on the nightstand beside her. Glanced at the window.

Oh.

Beams of sunlight were trying to infiltrate the blinds.

It must not be the middle of the night.

She twisted her head back toward the nightstand. Picked up her phone and peered at the screen.

It was eight-thirty in the morning—and Brad's name was flashing in the display.

She came instantly awake.

After accepting the call, she put the cell to her ear. "Good morning." She pushed back the covers, sat up, and swung her legs to the floor.

"Morning. Did I wake you?"

"Um…it was past time for me to get up anyway."

"That means yes." A sigh came over the line. "I'm sorry, Sam. I'm going into a meeting in a few minutes that could last most of the morning, and I knew I wouldn't be able to concentrate until I talked to you."

Her heart melted.

A guy who wouldn't be able to concentrate because he cared about her.

When had that ever happened in her world?

Like never.

Unfortunately, the wonderful feeling of being cherished had no future.

Tamping down a surge of dejection, she tried to call up a bright tone. "No apology necessary." She stood, squinting at the angry red welts and swelling on her ankle. At least the stinging sensation had dissipated.

"How are you feeling?"

"Better than yesterday." She limped toward the bathroom.

"That wouldn't take much. Can you give me a few more details?"

"Let's just say I won't be entering any races for a few days. My ankle's still kind of tender." She paused in front of the mirror over the vanity. Winced. "Nor will I be entering any beauty contests. But on the whole, I'm much improved over yesterday." A slight exaggeration, but she *was* feeling a bit better.

"I'm glad to hear that. But what a tough day. I still can't believe you were attacked by a swarm of bees."

"I assume that was a first for your church picnic."

"Yes. In fact, there have been a lot of firsts in the past twenty-four hours."

At the husky note in his voice, her pulse skittered.

He was talking about them. About the electricity. About the friendly date that had turned into so much more.

And she wasn't ready for that discussion.

"Um…I don't want to make you late for your meeting."

A few beats ticked by while she held her breath.

In the end, he followed her lead. "Yeah. I probably should get going. What's on your agenda for the day?"

"I have a showing at eleven, but I think I'm going to have

someone fill in for me." She returned to the bedroom and sat on the edge of the mattress.

"Smart idea. I'll check in with you later. I'd stop by tonight to get an in-person read on your condition, but I have a board meeting at church. Can we get together tomorrow for lunch or dinner?"

"I can't. I have a packed day during working hours, and I have my volunteer work in the evening."

He expelled a breath. "Wednesday's no good for me. I have to drive to KC for an afternoon meeting with a pastor who runs a program we're interested in implementing, and I won't be back until late. Could you do dinner on Thursday?"

"No. I'm taking a class on Thursday nights."

A few beats ticked by. "When did that start?"

"About a month ago."

"Something work-related?"

Sam bunched the sheet in her fingers.

If she told Brad about the Bible study class, he might think she was going just to please him, and that wasn't the case. It had been prompted more by a desire to fill the spiritual vacuum her life. And surprisingly enough it was helping.

"No. Just…personal interest."

Silence. As if he was waiting for her to offer more.

Dang.

She wasn't trying to shut him out, but her reawakening faith was too new and fragile to discuss with anyone.

However, his expectation that she'd offer a few details was clear evidence his feelings were running as deep as hers. And he'd be disappointed when she didn't.

Meaning she needed to give him the bad news as soon as possible, before anyone got hurt worse.

She swallowed, ignoring his implied question. "It sounds like we're both crazy busy this week. Are you available Friday for dinner?"

"Yes." No hesitation.

"Why don't you come here?" Because eating in would be more private. It could be hard to have the kind of conversation she was going to initiate in a restaurant.

"That works. Would you like me to pick up take-out?"

"No. I'll cook."

"Really? I didn't think you were into that."

"There are exceptions to every rule." Besides, after everything he'd done for her in the past twenty-four hours, he deserved a home-cooked meal. It also might help take the sting out of what she had to say. And how hard could it be to follow a recipe? Cooking wasn't rocket science, after all.

"Well, if you're sure, that would be great. I haven't had a home-cooked meal in a while. I'll call you before then, but what time sounds good?"

"Let's say seven." Two hours ought to be plenty of time to put together a nice meal.

"I'll be there. Talk to you soon."

As they said their goodbyes, another call beeped on her phone.

Laura.

Sam accepted that one too. "Hi, kiddo."

"You sound more like yourself today. How are you feeling?"

"Improving."

"Thank heaven. We were all so worried. Brad was beside himself."

She swung her legs back up onto the bed and plumped her pillow against the headboard. Leaned back. "Of course he was. I ruined his church picnic."

"That's not why he was upset, and you know it."

"Don't get any ideas."

"I'm not the one with ideas."

Sam frowned at the ceiling. Better nip this in the bud. "You're imagining things."

"No, I'm not. I saw how you two looked at each other yesterday. Everyone in the congregation did. There was enough electricity sparking between you to run the farm generator."

Sam closed her eyes.

No wonder she'd gotten so many appraising looks.

But admitting she was attracted to Brad would only spur Laura on.

"I intend to take all your observations with a grain of salt. As a new bride, you have a bad case of honeymoon-itis and are wearing rose-colored glasses."

"True—but I know what I saw. Nick saw it too. We had a long discussion about it last night."

"Laura…get real. I am *not* minister-girlfriend material." Best lay the groundwork for what was going to happen on Friday right now, before her BFF got too carried away.

"Why not?"

"You know why not."

"If you're thinking about any past indiscretions, Christianity is all about forgiveness."

Sam gave a mirthless laugh as she studied the welts marring the skin on her hand. "There's too much to forgive in my history."

"There's never too much. God always gives us a second chance."

"God, maybe. Man, not so much."

"You're underestimating Brad."

No, she wasn't. If her couple of lapses with men were the only issue, maybe he could overlook that.

But the secret she'd never shared with anyone was a different story. *That* indiscretion had had lethal consequences and left her riddled with guilt.

It had also convinced her she didn't deserve the kind of happy ending she'd always hoped Laura would find.

"Trust me, I would never underestimate Brad." Sam took a deep breath. "He's an amazing guy."

"Then give him a chance, Sam. You two seem right together."

"I think you need your eyesight checked. So how's the new landscaping job you landed at that swanky estate?"

Silence.

"You think I'm butting in, don't you?" Laura's frown was easy to hear in her voice.

"Yes. And that's okay. I gave you the third degree ad nauseum when you were dating Nick. After all, what are friends for?"

Laura's soft laugh came over the line. "I do remember that."

"Believe me, if there's ever anything to report on the romance front, I'll loop you in. But don't get your hopes up about me and Brad."

"A girl can dream, can't she? Will I see you Thursday night?"

"I'll be there."

"In the meantime, take care of yourself. And let me know if you need anything."

"I will. Thanks for checking in."

Once they ended the call, Sam set her cell back on the nightstand and examined her swollen ankle.

Bad as it looked, it would heal.

But the same couldn't be said about her heart.

In fact, after she said goodbye to Brad on Friday it might need CPR.

* * *

Some nights at the counseling center were easy. Some were hard.

This was a hard one.

Throat tightening, Sam leaned toward the distraught eighteen-year-old seated at a right angle to her and took her icy hand. This girl who was barely a woman was so in need of love and understanding. "You've told me what everyone else thinks, Jamie." She gentled her voice. "But what do *you* want to do?"

The teen chewed on her bottom lip as a tear trailed down her cheek. "I-I don't know. My mom and dad and John and all my friends say it will ruin my life if I have the baby, but it feels so...so wrong to just...get rid of it."

"I hear you. You'd like to believe there's not really a life at stake, because then your decision would be easy. But your heart is telling you there is, right?"

"Yeah. Exactly." Jamie sniffed.

Sam picked up the box of tissues from the table beside her and held it out to the young woman, choosing her words with care. "Has anyone suggested that it might ruin your life if you *don't* have the baby? If you 'get rid of it,' as you said?"

Her brow crinkled and she took a tissue. "No."

"You may want to ask yourself how you'll feel in a few years when you see a little child that would be the same age as your baby."

"But I'm not ready to be a mother. Especially a single mother." Jamie's tone grew more agitated, and desperation flared in her eyes. "John doesn't want any part of the baby. Neither do Mom and Dad. I'd be totally on my own."

"That's not true. The counseling center can offer you a lot of support. We can help with medical expenses, and I'm available to talk any time you need me. As for being a single mother, that's your choice. We'll assist in every way we can if you decide to take on that responsibility. But we have a list of dozens of couples who, for whatever reason, can't have their own children. They'd welcome your baby with open arms. We've given them a thorough vetting, and they're all fine people. So you can be confident your baby would have a wonderful home."

Jamie dabbed at her eyes. "I just feel so confused."

"That's understandable. It's a big decision, and it's hard to make a rational choice when you don't have support from family and friends. But remember, Jamie—you do have a choice."

After a moment, the young woman sighed. "I guess I'll think about it some more before I do anything."

That wasn't a win, but it was something.

"Good idea. In the meantime, I'm here if you need me." Sam reached for a notepad from the table and scrawled two numbers. "The top number is the counseling center." She tore off the sheet and handed it to her. "The bottom one is my cell. You can call me anytime, day or night, if you want to talk."

The teen took the piece of paper and tucked it into the pocket of her jeans. "Okay. And thanks for listening tonight. It helped a lot."

"I'm glad. In fact, why don't we set up another appointment for next week? I can give you more details on our program and answer any questions you might think of between now and then."

"I guess I could do that."

After they chose an agreeable time, Sam walked her to the door. "Take care, Jamie." She touched her arm. "And call me in a couple of days, just to chat. Will you do that?"

"Yeah. Thanks."

Sam watched the rail-thin young woman disappear down the

hall, then closed the door. Wandered back through the counseling center to the director's office.

Abigail looked up when she paused on the threshold. "How did it go?"

"I don't know." Sam massaged the bridge of her nose and sighed. "It's obvious she's trying to do the right thing, but it's also obvious she's not getting any support at home. I tried, but I'm not sure I got through to her."

Abigail folded her hands on her desk, compassion filling her eyes. "You did everything you could, Sam. That's all we can ask."

She stuck her hands into the pockets of her slacks. Fisted them. "I don't think it was enough. I have bad vibes about this one."

A couple of beats ticked by as Abigail studied her. "You know, sometimes I worry as much about you as the young women who come in here. You take this so much to heart, and I know it tears you up inside whenever you fail. Yet you keep coming back. I admire your dedication."

Sam waved aside the undeserved praise. "Don't admire me, Abigail. You know better." The director of the counseling center was the only person who knew even a piece of the tragic incident in her most dedicated volunteer's past.

"The main thing I know is that coming here week after week puts you through an emotional wringer. Whatever your motivation, it doesn't negate the good work you do. Thanks to you, a lot of children are here today—happy, healthy, and enjoying the gift of life."

Pressure built behind Sam's eyes. "But a lot of them aren't. And those are the ones who haunt me."

"My advice? Think about the ones who are. Otherwise, this work will beat you down." Abigail took a deep breath. Glanced at her watch. "Why don't you call it a night? You've already had a long session, and Pam is here. I don't expect we'll be inundated with walk-ins at this hour."

Not a bad idea. She wouldn't be of much use to another client tonight anyway, after the emotionally draining exchange with Jamie.

"If you don't mind, I'll take you up on that."

"Go." Abigail waved her off. "I'll see you next week."

"I'll be here."

"I know. You're our most reliable volunteer. Try to do something fun this weekend."

"I'll think about it."

But before Saturday morning dawned, she had something very unfun to do.

Namely, tell the man who was stealing her heart that there was no future for the two of them.

And that was going to be even harder than her session with Jamie.

8

The home-cooked dinner she'd promised Brad was a disaster. In fact, her whole Friday had been a disaster.

Sam shoved her hair back and rooted around for a knife in the kitchen drawer.

First a flat tire. Next, a difficult client who'd insisted on seeing a house at precisely one o'clock and then arrived half an hour late. That had been followed by a quicker-than-expected contract response, requiring an unscheduled stop at the office to do some paperwork.

And it didn't help that she'd tossed and turned last night after her unsettling session with Jamie at the counseling center.

Now she had a gourmet meal to prepare.

She dashed back to the recipe for chicken cordon bleu that she'd bookmarked a couple of days ago, now displayed front and center on her laptop screen in the kitchen.

As she reread it, her stomach clenched.

Maybe she'd been a tad too ambitious in her menu choices.

And maybe she should have familiarized herself with the recipes—beyond checking the ingredient list—before Friday at five o'clock.

No doubt Rachel could have whipped up the chicken, twice-baked potatoes, green beans almondine, and homemade biscuits in the window suggested in the recipes, but those times must be for people who knew what they were doing, not novices.

And she was definitely a novice.

At this rate, it was going to take her half a day to prepare the meal she'd planned.

At least she'd made the dessert last night after her stint at the counseling center, when she'd been too wired to sleep.

Sam frowned as she read the recipe for the entrée again.

How in the world did you flatten chicken breasts?

She tried pressing on them with the heel of her hand.

Zip.

Would a hammer work?

She dug one out of her tool drawer and gave the meat a whack.

Yes!

But the next step—layering the breasts with ham and cheese and then rolling them up—wasn't so easy.

She managed to get one of the uncooperative bundles into a semicylindrical shape, but it didn't look anything like the step-by-step pictures. And if she tried to dust it in flour, dip it in a beaten egg, and roll it in bread crumbs, it was going to fall apart.

Oh, mercy.

What had she gotten herself into?

She plowed ahead anyway, then moved on to the potatoes. At least she'd put them in the oven the minute she'd gotten home.

But when she removed them and tried to slice off a long end so she could scoop out the interior, the skin was hard as a rock.

She double-checked the recipe.

Bake for one hour and fifteen minutes at four hundred degrees.

That's what she'd done, wasn't it?

She zipped back to the oven and squinted at the temperature gauge.

It read five hundred, not four hundred.

Groaning, she closed her eyes.

This was *not* how she'd planned her meal prep to go. And she was running out of time.

She sucked in a breath. Picked up the pen next to her menu list and crossed off the biscuits. They were so not happening.

Mashing her lips together, she tackled the potatoes again and eventually managed to cut through the crusty skin. But in the process, much of the shell shattered. Nevertheless, she scooped out the shriveled insides, added the other ingredients, and put the mixture in what was left of the skins.

On to the beans.

She scanned that recipe.

The sauce sounded easy enough—just onion and slivered almonds sautéed in butter.

After chopping the onion, she dumped everything into a small frying pan and set the heat on low.

Maybe now she could change out of the T-shirt and leggings she'd thrown on when she'd arrived home and into something nicer and flour-free. She also needed to touch up her makeup and comb her hair.

Five minutes later, when the harsh shriek of the smoke detector blasted through the condo, her hand jerked as she was repairing her eyeliner.

What in the world?

Dropping the tube of makeup into the sink, she dashed toward the kitchen, heart pounding. Paused for a brief second on the threshold to scan the room.

It took her only a moment to spot the source of the problem.

Smoke was seeping out of the oven.

She raced that direction, yanked open the door, and reared back as a billowing gray cloud engulfed her.

Coughing, she tried to wave the smoke away as she peered inside.

Near as she could determine, the cheese had leaked out of the chicken breasts and was now burning.

She grabbed the pan and removed it, turned on the exhaust fan, opened a window, and began waving a towel at the smoke detector to clear the air.

When the piercing alarm finally fell silent, Sam wilted against the counter, surveying the sad-looking chicken.

How could she salvage that unappetizing mess?

Maybe if she scooped the cheese back in and—

She froze. Sniffed. Glanced toward the stove.

The almonds and onions in her butter sauce were turning black.

Oh, geez.

What else could go wrong?

She flew across the room and removed the pan from the heat before the smoke alarm went off again. Gazed at the potatoes waiting to go into the oven. They looked pathetic too. The skins were on the verge of disintegrating, and the filling was already spilling out.

Now what?

Was it too late to call the nearby gourmet shop and order dinner for—

Ding-dong.

Her stomach bottomed out.

It couldn't be seven already, could it?

She peeked at her watch.

Yes, it was. And Brad was punctual, as usual.

She eyed the door to her patio, fighting the temptation to sneak out and disappear.

But that was the coward's way out.

There was nothing to do but face him and admit defeat.

Her shoulders sagged.

So much for her plan to soften the news she had to share with a memorable meal.

A *pleasantly* memorable meal, not one memorable for all the wrong reasons.

The bell rang again, and she forced her legs to carry her toward the door. Took a deep breath. Pulled it open.

Brad, of course, looked great in his pristine tan slacks and an open-necked pinstripe shirt. He was also carrying a bottle of wine.

They were both going to need that before this night was over.

Brad's smile of welcome faded as he gave her a once-over. "Are you okay?"

"Sure. Fine. Why wouldn't I be? I mean, how hard can it be to prepare a dinner for two?" Her voice cracked as a note of hysteria crept into her voice.

Furrows dented his brow. "May I come in?"

"Yes. Of course." She backed up and ushered him through the door.

He entered, but paused in the foyer as she shut the door behind him. "Are the stings still giving you trouble?"

He thought her manic state was related to the stings?

Not even close.

A frenzied day, a kitchen disaster, an upsetting evening and restless night, and a looming bombshell would throw anyone off their game.

But it was easier to blame her agitated state on bees.

"They aren't healing quite as fast as I'd hoped."

"You shouldn't be trying to cook dinner."

Pressure built behind her eyes, and she blinked to clear her vision. "Trying is an apt word. It's a disaster."

"Tell me what happened." His voice was caring, his eyes concerned.

"I ruined our dinner."

"I don't mind if everything's not perfect."

He wasn't getting her message.

"It's not just not perfect, Brad. It's inedible."

"It can't be that bad."

"Yes it can. Trust me. It's not a pretty picture in my kitchen." She took a deep breath. "I wanted to treat you to a home-cooked meal, but I don't spend much time in the kitchen. I didn't realize the recipes I chose would be so time-consuming or involved. I'm sure it's something R-Rachel could have whipped up without breaking a sweat, but it was beyond me. I'm s-sorry."

He took her hand. Twined his fingers with hers in a firm, comforting grip. "Relax. It's not the end of the world. We'll make do. What turned out the best?"

"Dessert. And it's not just the *best*. It's the *only* thing that turned out."

He studied her for a moment. "Then let's go with Plan B. While you clean up the kitchen, I'll run down to the Italian place a few blocks from here and get dinner for us."

"But I promised you a home-cooked meal."

"Can I tell you something? A home-cooked meal would have been nice, but food isn't the reason I came tonight." He smiled and squeezed her fingers.

Her heart flip-flopped.

That was good news on the dinner front, but it only reminded her of the other problem she needed to tackle tonight.

Brad released her fingers and moved back to the door. "I shouldn't be gone long. Will you be all right?"

"Yes." When his eyes narrowed, she forced up the corners of her mouth. "I'll be fine."

After a moment, he nodded. "Okay. Is lasagna okay, or would you rather have something else?"

"I like lasagna."

"Then that's what I'll order. I'll be back soon."

As the door clicked shut behind him, Sam exhaled. Massaged her temple as she considered her priorities.

Personal clean-up definitely took precedence over kitchen clean-up.

She pivoted, dashed for her bedroom, and examined herself in the full-length mirror in her closet.

Oh, mercy.

She was a wreck.

No wonder Brad had looked alarmed.

This barefoot, flour-bedecked woman with the disheveled hair and long black stripe of eyeliner veering east from her right eye looked nothing like the put-together career woman Brad knew.

Maybe the two of them had no future together, but this was *not* the image she wanted him to remember when he looked back on their time together.

Shifting into warp speed, she combed her hair, repaired her makeup, and changed into a silk blouse, black skirt, and flats.

Once more she examined her reflection.

Better.

Now she could try to restore some semblance of order to the kitchen before Brad returned.

And work on the explanation she was going to give him after dinner about why it wasn't a good idea for them to see each other anymore.

* * *

Something was up.

And it wasn't leaving him with a warm and fuzzy feeling.

As Brad waited for his order in a corner of the restaurant lobby, he propped a shoulder against the wall, folded his arms, and tried to make sense of what had just transpired at her condo.

Why would a recipe or two gone awry push a woman who took everything in stride to the brink of hysteria?

It didn't make sense.

But maybe her remark about Rachel had something to do with it.

If she was beginning to think romance was in the air, she might be comparing herself to the image he'd painted of a perfect wife. One with a similar background to his, who was well-suited to the role of minister's wife.

It was possible Sam thought her reputation and limited domestic abilities disqualified her for that job. That she fell short of the lofty standards she assumed were required.

Truth be told, his perceptions about her history and the difference in their approach to life had thrown him in the beginning too. The two of them hadn't seemed like a logical match.

Yet the more he'd gotten to know her, the more certain he was they had potential.

The challenge was convincing her of that.

Tonight, however, wasn't the time to launch his campaign. Not in her frazzled state.

Best plan? Keep the evening low-key and casual. Don't do anything to rush her. Give her breathing space to adjust to the idea of a pairing. Because pressure of any kind could spook her. He needed to buy himself time to build his case, until their compatibility became as obvious to her as it was to him.

And he had the perfect tool at hand. It was almost providential

Twenty minutes later, when he rang her bell again, he had a definitive strategy in place.

The lock clicked, and as the door opened he gave her a fast but thorough sweep.

Makeup impeccable, hair perfect, clothes that bore no trace of flour or breadcrumbs. And the frenzy in her eyes had subsided.

Better.

Even if there was a lingering trace of…trepidation?…in her irises.

He smiled and held up the large bag. "Dinner is served."

"Smells delicious." She motioned him in. "Let's divvy it up and dive in."

She led him to her dining room, where the table was set with a linen cloth, china dishes, and crystal glasses. His bottle of wine had been opened, and a bouquet of fresh flowers took the place of honor in the center.

"Nice."

"I may have failed in the kitchen, but I do know how to set a table."

The two of them plated the entrées, the salad, and the bread, then took their places.

"Do you mind if I say a blessing?" He draped his napkin over his lap.

"I wouldn't expect any less from a man of the cloth."

Instead of taking her hand, as he was tempted to do, he linked his fingers, rested them on the edge of the table, and offered a simple prayer that focused on food, fellowship, and friendship.

Emphasis on friendship, which earned him a side-eye that registered in his peripheral vision.

Good. She'd noticed.

Because it was becoming clear that Sam wasn't ready to commit to anything more.

Fine by him. He was a patient man.

"That was very nice." She set her own napkin in her lap and picked up her fork. "This smells far more appetizing than the charred food in my trash can."

"Maybe it wasn't as bad as you thought. Blackened is all the rage, after all."

"Blackened, yes. Burnt, no." She broke off a bite of lasagna with her fork. Tasted it. "Mmm. I haven't had Italian for a while."

"Me, neither. So tell me about your day—before the cooking catastrophe."

She wrinkled her nose. "It wasn't much better."

As she proceeded to give him a blow-by-blow of her difficult client in her usual gregarious style, some of the tension in the air dissipated.

For the remainder of the meal, he kept the conversation focused on impersonal topics—but when it was time for dessert, a bit of anxiety crept back into her demeanor.

She was gearing up to tell him something he didn't want to hear.

As she reached for his plate, he touched her hand. "Could we sit for a few minutes before dessert? That was a heavy meal."

Her gaze flicked to his hand. Darted away. "The dessert is light. I made a trifle. It looks good, but I make no guarantees about the taste." She offered him a smile that seemed forced.

"I have a feeling it's fine. And a dessert like that I can handle. But first I wanted to pass some information on to you."

She cocked her head, her expression curious but cautious. "Okay."

"Dad's birthday is coming up. It's a big one, and Rebecca and I managed to convince him to let us throw a small party. We've been working on the guest list this week. He wants us to send you an invitation."

Her features softened. "That's so sweet of him."

"He tells me you two have become pen pals."

Her lips bowed. "I wouldn't go that far, but we do email. Always about gardening."

"In case you haven't figured it out, he's become a fan."

"The feeling is mutual."

"I'm glad—but I hope he's not becoming a nuisance."

She dismissed that with a flip of her hand. "Not at all. He's a lovely man, and I enjoy talking flowers with him."

"So would you be willing to come to the party? I know you're busy, but it would mean a lot to him."

Faint puckers appeared on her brow. "When is it?"

"In three weeks." He gave her the date. "It won't be anything super fancy. Just a luncheon at Rebecca's restaurant in Ste. Genevieve for about forty people. She's closed on Mondays, which is why we chose that date. We'll also have a three-piece combo. As Dad always says, it's not a party without music. I realize that's a workday for you, but if you could swing it Dad would be thrilled."

Her lips twisted into a wry grin. "Every day is a workday for realtors. Let me check my schedule while I dish up our desserts. You ready to put your stomach at risk?"

"I'm not worried."

"You would be if you'd seen my kitchen before I got rid of the evidence." She rose and picked up his plate. "I bet Rachel was a wonderful cook."

Another reference to his wife.

Either Sam felt intimidated by her, or she was trying to squelch any burgeoning romantic interest he might have in a new woman by bringing up the woman he'd wed.

Her discouragement tactic, if that's what it was, wasn't going to work, but he could try to dispel any feelings of inferiority.

"Rachel was talented in the kitchen." He kept his tone conversational. "But I've found that everyone has their own unique talent. For example, you have a wonderful gift for drawing people out and lifting their spirits. I can speak from personal experience on that one."

Sam repositioned her almost empty wineglass, keeping her gaze averted. "Not a very practical skill, though."

"Depends on how you define practical. Joy and happiness are great buffers for the trials and tribulations of everyday life. That seems practical to me."

Unless he was mistaken, a faint hint of pink appeared on her cheeks before she turned away, plates in hand, and headed for the kitchen. "Give me a few minutes to make coffee and get our dessert ready."

As she disappeared and silence descended, Brad leaned back. Twirled the stem of his wineglass.

Thank goodness he'd had Dad's party invitation in his back pocket to try to defer any Dear John speech she may have been planning for tonight.

Assuming it worked—and she agreed to attend—sometime in the next three weeks he needed to figure out why she was so gun-shy about the two of them.

Because lack of interest wasn't the reason.

He might have been out of the romance game for a while, but a man didn't lose his ability to read attraction in a woman's eyes—and it was front and center in Sam's.

So between now and the party, he had to get some answers.

Which meant he needed to see her on a regular basis.

He took the last sip of his wine. Leaned back.

If she intended to pull back on their relationship, she might find excuses to refuse dates. Which could complicate things.

His lips tipped up ever so slightly.

Except he had a sure-fire way to convince her to spend time with him.

* * *

This evening wasn't going anything like she'd planned—on so many levels.

First the food fiasco, then Brad's references to friendship, then the invitation to his dad's party.

Sam started the coffeemaker. Blew out a breath.

The food situation had been glossed over, thanks to the empathetic man waiting for her in the dining room.

His friendship comments, however, had thrown her.

Had she misread his interest all along?

Maybe.

After all, the heat in his eyes when she'd sprawled all over him after they fell in the three-legged race could happen with any guy—minister or not—if a woman got that up close and personal with him. And his tender, kind manner and care after the bee incident could have been fueled more by guilt than anything. As his guest, she was his responsibility.

She crossed to the fridge, pulled out the bowl of trifle, and spooned two servings into bowls.

Bottom line?

Maybe she didn't have to give the speech she'd prepared.

Maybe she could wait and see if any more signs of romance appeared.

And if she didn't have to break things off with Brad tonight—if friendship really was all he had on his mind—what could be the harm in going to Henry's party?

Or was she letting the two glasses of wine she'd downed muddle her thinking?

Who knew at this point?

So she'd just have to wing it for the rest of the evening.

Sam poured the coffee and placed it on a tray, then added the bowls of trifle, cream, and sugar.

When she reentered the dining room, Brad rose while she set the tray on the table. "The dessert looks good."

"I guess we'll find out." She put a bowl in each place and retook her seat. Brad did likewise, adding a splash of cream to his coffee before dipping his spoon into the creamy dessert and taking a generous sample.

"You're braver than I am." She scooped up a tiny bite. "I have ice cream in the freezer if this is an epic fail."

He put the spoon in his mouth, and she watched as he chewed. But his expression told her nothing.

"Well?" She leaned forward.

"It's delicious." He smiled and took another spoonful. "Try it."

She followed his lead. "Wow. This is actually tasty."

"More than." He kept eating. "You can make this for me anytime. In fact, I'd forfeit dinner for a bowl of your trifle."

"I'm glad at least *one* thing turned out."

"I think the whole evening turned out fine. A perfect way to end a long week."

"Even if you had to supply the dinner?"

"Even if." He took a sip of his coffee. "How goes your search for a house for me? You haven't said anything about that tonight."

"The market's tight at the moment. I'm not seeing much that meets the parameters you laid out."

"Maybe I'll have to adjust those."

"No." She shook her head and met his gaze. "Don't settle. You'll only regret it." Whether it was a house or a woman—just in case he still had any amorous inclinations toward her.

"Sometimes it's smart to adjust expectations." His mild expression and tone didn't suggest there was any deeper meaning to his comment, nor did his follow-up. "I might be able to bend on some of the cosmetic features I want, but a fireplace is a must."

"Noted."

"I'll start keeping a closer eye on the listings too. Maybe something will catch my eye."

Did he think she wasn't being diligent enough?

"I do look at them every day for you." As she finished her dessert, she brought him up to speed on the latest offerings she'd considered—and rejected.

"I appreciate your diligence, but two heads and all that." He glanced at his watch. "It sounds like we both had a busy week. I don't know about you, but I'm about ready to call it a night."

At eight-thirty?

She tried to mask her surprise.

Heck, in her bar-hopping days she'd just been getting started at this hour.

But an eat-and-run evening was another indication Brad had no romantic intentions for this get-together, and that was a good thing...even if a foolish pang of disappointment echoed in her heart. On the bright side, though, as long as things remained light and friendly between them, she could continue to see him.

Besides, thanks to her restless sleep last night exhaustion was beginning to nick away at her energy.

"I plan to make an early night of it myself." She set her cup on the table.

"May I help with the clean-up?" He swept a hand over the table.

"No. You provided the food. That's enough of a contribution for the evening." She stood.

He rose too. After setting his napkin on the table, he strolled toward the door. "I'll call you with details about Dad's party, but I guarantee he'll be over the moon that you're attending."

"Tell him I wouldn't miss it." She stopped a few feet away as he paused at the door and turned toward her. "Thanks for being so understanding about tonight. And for bringing wine."

"Disasters happen. Remind me to tell you sometime about the sermon I gave at a funeral once early in my ministry when I used the wrong name for the deceased through the entire thing."

She winced, even as warmth spread through her at his humility and lack of pretense. "That must have been super embarrassing."

"It was. I didn't even realize what I'd done until I overheard two of the attendees talking at the reception afterward. I wanted to sink through the floor."

"But you lived to tell the tale."

"I did. And what I learned from my faux pas was that most of the things we think are a big deal don't turn out to be in hindsight."

But some did.

She managed to hold on to her smile. "It was a painful lesson, though."

"True. And I never forgot it. To this day I write the deceased's name in large block letters and put it on the pulpit before every funeral." He winked, which sent a wave of warmth coursing through her. "I'll let you get to the clean-up." He glanced toward the kitchen. "Or should we call in FEMA?"

She made a face at him as she moved toward the door. "Ha ha. It's not *that* bad."

"Mission accomplished. Perspective is restored." He grinned and tapped the tip of her nose with his finger. "I'll be in touch. Sleep well."

He twisted the knob, exited, and pulled the door shut behind him.

For a full minute after he left, Sam remained where she was, waiting for her pulse to slow as she gently touched her nose.

This was so much better than how she'd expected tonight to end.

Thanks to Brad's kindness, consideration, and casual, easygoing manner, her stress level had been dropping all evening.

Nevertheless, as she turned to tackle the mess in the kitchen she faced the truth.

Brad might have relegated their relationship to the just-friends category, but the more she saw of him the more she *wanted* to see of him.

And not just as friends.

So while she'd stick with him until she found the house of his dreams, once that happened she'd have to call it quits between them.

Otherwise, a broken heart was in her future.

Guaranteed.

9

A nother house?

Sam frowned as she read the text from Brad.

> This one might be worth looking at. Do you have any time late today? Say around five? I'll be tied up at the office until then. I'll bribe you with dinner afterward to sweeten the deal if necessary. ☺

She clicked on the listing link.

Like the other two he'd sent since their Italian dinner at her condo twelve days ago, it didn't fit the clean-lines/large-windows/open-floor-plan/integration-with-nature parameters he'd specified in their initial meeting. While the Cape Cod bungalow was cute, it was nothing like the mid-century modern style she'd been hunting for.

But it was possible she'd misread his tastes. And if he wanted to view houses she would never have picked for him, she'd oblige. That was her job.

She angled away from the seller's disclosure for a new listing that she was reviewing on her laptop and put her thumbs to work.

> No problem. Five works. Meet you there. No bribe necessary.

Not that she wouldn't enjoy dinner with him. Just like she'd enjoyed the coffee stop during their first house-hunting outing.

But dinner was a different animal. More intimate. Why introduce a setting that could stir up romantic fantasies on one or both sides, when everything was going so well on the friendship front?

The rest of the day was a whirl, as usual, and she had to race to get to the house Brad wanted to see, running a few yellow lights along the way. As it was, she arrived five minutes late.

But it didn't matter. He wasn't there yet.

Huh.

That was a first.

Brad was never, ever late.

She parked in the driveway, pulled out her cell, and checked messages.

No text, no email, no voicemail.

Maybe he was tied up in traffic and didn't want to risk an accident by pulling out his cell.

Nevertheless, a vague niggle of unease skittered through her.

When he still hadn't arrived fifteen minutes later, her unease inched toward panic.

It was time to text him.

She pulled out her cell and typed in a quick note.

At the house. Everything okay?

Five minutes passed.

Ten.

Fifteen.

Nada.

Okay, this was weird. And scary.

She tapped a finger on the steering wheel.

He'd said he'd be at the office until he left for the showing. Could he still be there? Should she drive over and check, just in case there was a problem? What if he'd fallen or something? Hit his head. Broken a leg. After all, those things did happen. And his church was only ten minutes from here.

Without further debate, she twisted the key in the ignition, backed out of the driveway, and sped toward the church.

Once she arrived, she swung into the lot and parked near the office. Strode toward the door and turned the knob.

It was locked.

She blew out a breath.

Had he gone to the adjacent parsonage?

She hurried over to that door, rang the bell—and struck out there too.

Propping her hands on her hips, she surveyed the grounds.

Was he even on the premises?

If there was a window in the garage, she might be able to see if his car was here.

She circled the attached structure.

Yes!

There was a small window on one side.

Clenching the strap of her shoulder bag, she picked up her pace. Paused beside the window and cupped her hands around the glass.

His car was inside.

Meaning he was here.

But where was he?

She scanned the property, homing in on the church.

There wouldn't be any services at this hour on a weekday, but her instincts told her that's where she'd find him.

As she walked toward the church, a feeling of dread welled up inside her, clawing at her windpipe.

Something felt...off.

When she reached the door, she hesitated.

Whatever was inside wasn't going to be happy. Or easy to deal with.

But if Brad was alone and needed the comforting presence of a friend, she wasn't going to let bad vibes chase her away.

She tugged on the door, and when it opened without protest she stepped inside.

The vestibule was empty, so she moved to the double doors that led to the church proper. Gently eased one open and slipped in.

It took a few moments for her eyes to acclimate to the dimness, but once they did she scanned the church. Frowned.

It seemed to be empty.

But it wasn't.

Brad was here. She could *feel* his presence.

She gave the church another, slower sweep.

If he hadn't reached up to run a hand over his face just as her gaze moved past, she'd have missed him on her second pass too.

Gripping the back of the last pew, she studied him as her pulse tapped out a staccato beat.

Head bowed, shoulders slumped, he sat near the front, off to one side, half-hidden in the shadows. Defeat and sadness radiated from him, as did darkness and desolation, as palpable as the textured iron door handle had been beneath her fingers moments ago.

A cold knot formed in her stomach.

Something bad had happened. Very bad. And Brad had sought solace here, with God.

She drew a shaky breath.

Maybe three was a crowd in a situation like this. Maybe he needed to be alone and would consider her presence an intrusion.

It might be best if she waited outside until he emerged.

But just as she started to turn away, a choked, ragged sound echoed softly in the church. One she recognized all too well from personal experience.

It was a sob.

Decision made.

He was hurting, and she wanted to help. It was as simple as that.

Taking a deep breath, she groped through her purse for her cell. Put it on silent mode to eliminate any interruptions so she could give him her total focus. Then she moved forward, pausing a few steps behind him. "Brad?" When he didn't respond to her soft summons, she tried again, raising her volume a few decibels.

He lifted his head and looked toward her.

A shock wave shuddered through her.

Wretched wasn't a word she dusted off often, but it was the only one in her vocabulary that came anywhere close to describing his face. His dazed eyes were haunted and filled with despair. His skin was stretched taut across his cheekbones. The deep grooves etched in his brow were echoed in the brackets beside his mouth. And the hand he lifted to massage his temples was beyond shaky.

Trying to quell her burgeoning panic, Sam moved closer and sank down on the pew beside him. "Brad, what's wrong?"

He blinked, as if trying to focus. "Sam? Why are you here?"

"We were supposed to tour a house. When you didn't show up, I got worried and came looking for you."

"House?" His face went blank.

132

She swallowed past the fear clogging her throat, keeping her voice as calm as she could. "Yes. You said it caught your eye. That it might be one you'd consider buying."

He frowned, and his eyes cleared bit by bit, as if he was mentally shifting gears. "I completely forgot. I'm sorry."

"Don't worry about it. The house isn't going anywhere. Just tell me what happened." She took a steadying breath and braced. "Is it your dad? Is he all right?"

"Yes. He's fine."

When he didn't offer any more information, she twined her fingers with his. "Then what's wrong? Can you tell me?"

His grip on her hand tightened to the point of pain, but she didn't wince. If he needed a lifeline to grasp, she was happy to provide it.

"I don't want to burden you with my problems."

"Brad, I care about you. And friends are there for each other. Please. Let me help."

His expression grew desolate. "It's too late to help."

"But it's never too late for someone to listen. So talk to me. Tell me what happened."

He glanced toward the sanctuary. After a few moments, he swallowed. Exhaled. "Remember I told you once that I tend to get too involved in the lives of my congregation? Take things too personally? Well, today is an example of the downside of that."

"What happened?"

He wiped his free hand down his face. "There's a middle-aged couple in the congregation with a teenage son who has issues. I've been counseling them for the past few weeks. Based on everything they said I came to the conclusion last week that he could be clinically depressed and that they needed to get him professional help. But I made that recommendation too late. He committed suicide this morning." His voice rasped, and he dipped his head.

Her stomach knotted.

No wonder he looked so bleak and broken.

"Oh, Brad. I'm so sorry." She laid her cheek against his shoulder, searching for words of comfort. But what could you say in the face of such tragedy and sorrow?

His whole body was shaking, and grief emanated from every pore as he spoke. "What kind of minister am I that I couldn't prevent a tragedy like this?" Anguish scored his voice.

She frowned.

He was questioning his ministry, blaming himself for that boy's death?

That was wrong in every possible way.

She straightened up and angled toward him. "Brad, look at me." She waited until his despondent eyes focused on her. "You are a fine man and a fine minister." Her tone was fierce, and that was okay. She wanted her message to sink in. "Your only problem is that you care too much. Are the parents blaming you for their son's death?"

"I don't know. But *I* blame me. I should have realized sooner that he needed help. And when they called today, looking for comfort, I failed them then too. When I visited them, I had no answer to their question about why a young life would be wasted. All I could do was sit with them, say how sorry I am, and remind them that God's ways are often difficult to understand."

"Maybe that's what they needed to hear." She gentled her voice.

He shook his head. "A minister should be able to do more than that. To find better words to ease pain."

"But ministers are also human. You did the best you could, and that's all anyone can ask."

He exhaled. "Maybe. But it doesn't bring their son back." He was still clutching her hand, but his grip had loosened a tad, and his tremors were subsiding.

"No, it doesn't. But guilt won't either. Maybe you need to give this to God and let it go." They'd talked about that in her last Bible class, and it had been on her mind ever since.

A ghost of a smile touched his lips. "You're the one who sounds like a preacher."

"Hardly." She shook her head. "How long have you been sitting here?"

"I don't know. What time is it?"

"Almost six."

"Two hours, I guess. I came here as soon as I got back."

"Did you have lunch?"

"No. I went over to be with the parents when they called around noon."

"You need to eat."

He shook his head. "I'm not hungry."

"You still need to eat. What do you have on hand in your house, besides frozen dinners?"

"The basics. Eggs, cheese, bread, milk, cereal."

"Before you panic, I'm not going to offer to cook anything elaborate. But I can whip up a decent omelet. Let me make one for you." Because if she didn't, he wouldn't eat tonight. She'd lay odds on that.

A hint of warmth took the edge off the sadness in his eyes. "You don't have to do that."

"I *want* to." She stood. "Come on. Let me do this for you."

After a moment, he rose. "To tell you the truth, I'm more in need of company than food."

"Well, with me you'll get two for the price of one."

He didn't talk much while she prepared a simple meal for both of them. But he stayed close. As if her mere presence was comforting to him.

He didn't seem in the mood to converse while they ate at his kitchen table, either, so she didn't push him.

After they finished, he smiled at her across the table. "I do feel a little better now that I've eaten. Thank you. For everything."

"I didn't do much."

"You were here when I needed you. That means a lot."

"I'm glad I could help." She rose and began clearing the table. "I saw a gallon of ice cream in the freezer. Would you like some for dessert?"

"No, but feel free if you're in the mood." He stood too and picked up their water glasses.

"I'm full. I'll just help you clean up and then take off." When he didn't respond, she turned from the sink to find him frowning at her. "What's wrong?"

The furrows on his brow disappeared and he lifted one shoulder as he joined her at the sink, their glasses in hand. "I was just thinking that it would be nice if you could stay for a while. Maybe watch a movie or TV with me. Nothing taxing. No heavy conversation. But I'm sure you've had a busy day."

Yes, she had.

And hanging around the parsonage alone with him carried a whiff of danger. Even if they only watched a movie together, and even if the suggestion had been prompted by tragedy, an evening like that had overtones of a date.

In all fairness, though, after the events of the past few hours Brad wasn't likely to get any romantic notions. And leaving him alone after his terrible day seemed uncaring.

"I could stay for a couple of hours."

He gave her a grateful smile. "Thanks."

They tidied up the kitchen, then checked out the offerings on TV. Lucked into a classic comedy.

But halfway through Brad fell asleep beside her, his head resting on the back of the couch as his eyelids fluttered…then drifted closed. Seconds later his even breathing confirmed that exhaustion had triumphed over any interest he might have in the action on the screen.

No surprise after the emotional toll this day had taken on him.

Sam reached for the remote, turned down the volume—and turned her attention to the man beside her, the harsh lines of anguish in his face now softened in sleep.

Pressure built in her throat as she traced his strong profile with her gaze.

Being here with him felt so right. Like this was meant to be. Like they were supposed to be a couple.

Only they weren't.

This was a one-off, nothing more. One friend comforting another in a time of sorrow. And when the movie ended, she'd nudge him awake if necessary and say good night.

In the meantime, though, why not enjoy being with him?

Catching her lower lip between her teeth, she scooted a tad closer and tentatively brushed his hair back from his forehead.

When he sighed, she jerked her hand back.

But before she could scoot away, he shifted his position, and his head dropped to her shoulder.

Whoops.

She ought to wake him. Leave.

But with his warm breath caressing the hollow of her throat, she didn't have the strength to walk away. Not just yet.

Instead, she tilted her head until his hair brushed her cheek. Closed her eyes.

Heaven.

If only it could last.

But she had this moment, and she'd stretch it out as long as she could.

The movie ended, and she turned off the TV. The sun set, and the room dimmed. Her own eyelids grew heavy. Too heavy to prop up.

Fine.

She'd take a quick catnap. And then she'd go home.

* * *

As the pressure against his chest registered, Brad opened his eyes.

Only faint illumination spilled into the room from the low-wattage bulb in the lamp on the table in the foyer behind him.

What was that weight on...

He froze as a familiar spicy, exotic scent tickled his nostrils. Angled his head and squinted at the woman nestled against him, her hand splayed against his chest, her nose nestled into his neck, and her glorious hair spilling over her shoulder.

Sam was asleep beside him on the couch.

For a long moment he studied her.

She looked different in slumber. Younger. More vulnerable. And oh-so-appealing.

Too appealing.

If he wanted to continue playing the friendship card, he needed to extricate himself. Because his thoughts right now went way beyond friendship.

Wake her up, Matthews.

Right.

He tried taking a few deep breaths to slow his pulse, but when it refused to cooperate he finally gave her a gentle nudge. "Hey, sleepyhead."

Instead of waking up, she gave a contented sigh and burrowed closer to him. Like that was where she belonged.

And he was pretty sure she did.

But she needed to come to that conclusion too—when she was awake.

He tried another prod, this one with a bit more force. "Sam. Wake up."

After a moment her eyes flickered open and she gave him a groggy stare. "What time is it?" Her voice was thick and a bit slurred.

She'd obviously been in a deep slumber.

"I don't know. You're leaning on my arm, and it's asleep."

Her eyes cleared, and she shot into an upright position as color flooded her face. "Sorry about that. I guess we both drifted off."

"Don't be sorry. I expect we both needed the sleep." He shook his arm to get the blood flowing, then angled his wrist. Hiked up his eyebrows. "To answer your question, it's twelve-thirty." Long past the hour propriety would deem appropriate for a woman to be in a minister's house. "I hate to end this slumber party, but no matter how innocent the circumstances, I doubt my congregation would approve of a woman being here this late at night."

She pushed herself to her feet. "Of course not. I'm sorry I put you in a compromising position. Let me grab my purse from the kitchen and I'll take off."

Before he could stop her, she dashed for the back of the house.

When she returned, he was waiting for her in the foyer. "I'll walk you out."

"No need."

"Yes, there is. Good manners were drilled into me by both Mom and Dad." He twisted the doorknob. "Shall we?"

She hesitated, but only for a moment. "I wouldn't want you to disappoint your parents."

A mist hung in the air outside, lending an otherworldly feel to their surroundings as they walked through the midnight darkness to where she'd left her car in front of the church office. Halfway there, he took her arm on the pretext of guiding her over a section of rough pavement. An unnecessary gesture, since the property was adequately lit, but the limited light was a good excuse to initiate the physical contact.

She didn't object.

When they reached her car, she turned toward him. "Will you be okay here by yourself?"

"Yes. Thanks to you."

"No." She shook her head. "You just needed company tonight, and I was available. Any person with an ounce of compassion would have sufficed."

Did she really believe that?

If so, he needed to correct her conclusion.

"Not true." He took her hand. Folded her fingers in his as she raised startled eyes to his. "Only you could have brought me a measure of peace."

Her breath hitched as she locked gazes with him. "I guess...I guess that's what friends are for."

Hmm.

Maybe he'd overplayed the friends notion.

And maybe it was time to ease that to the next level.

"What you did tonight went way beyond friendship." He stroked his thumb over the back of her hand. "You're very special to me, Sam."

She moistened her lips. "Y-you're special to me too."

"Can I be honest with you?"

Indecision flared in her eyes, so vivid it was discernible even in the dim light. "I suppose so."

"I wish you could stay here all night. But since that's not possible, at least let me send you off with a proper goodbye."

He took a step closer to her, until only a whisper separated them. Lifted his hand and gently cupped her cheek in his palm, watching her face. One sign of doubt, one ounce of resistance, one hint of rejection and he'd back off.

But he got none of those.

So he dipped his head and pressed his lips against hers.

For a moment, she didn't move a muscle. And then her mouth stirred beneath his. Tentative. Seeking. Exploring.

It was nothing like the kind of kiss he'd expected from a woman with Sam's experience.

It was almost...shy.

And very, very endearing.

When he backed off, she groped for the car behind her, as if she needed to steady herself.

He could relate.

Simple as the kiss had been, it had packed a wallop. And left him wanting more.

Much more.

"Text me when you get home?" His request came out in a hoarse rasp.

"It will be late." Her whispered response was barely there.

"I'll be up." No doubt for hours after that adrenaline-pumping and imagination-stirring kiss.

"Okay." She sucked in a breath, swiveled around, and slid behind the wheel of her car.

As she started the engine and pulled away from the parsonage, he shoved his hands into his pockets, lips still tingling from the pressure of her mouth on hers. And he stayed there until her taillights disappeared in the mist.

Maybe he'd made a mistake by kissing her tonight.

But for the life of him, he couldn't conjure up a single regret.

10

Their kiss had changed everything.

Every nerve in her body still vibrating after the delicious feel of Brad's lips against hers, Sam squeezed the wheel as she drove through the dark, empty streets between the parsonage and her condo.

The kiss hadn't been toe-tingling passionate, but it hadn't been a chaste peck, either. Brad had romance on his mind.

And kissing him back had been a mistake.

It wasn't as if she'd *had* to respond. He'd given her an opportunity to pull back, hovering over her lips as he searched her face. All she'd had to do was retreat a step or turn aside.

But she hadn't.

Because she'd wanted that kiss as much as he had.

And since they'd crossed into new territory, it was time to face the truth she'd been dancing around.

She was head over heels for a man who deserved a much better woman than her. Someone far more worthy of him.

Now what?

She flipped on her blinker and hung a right, changing direction.

Henry's party was in a week. She couldn't back out on that and disappoint Brad's father. Nor could she cast a damper over the event by telling Brad before then that she wouldn't be seeing him anymore except on a professional level.

So she'd have to avoid him until it was over. If he wanted to tour any more houses in the interim, she'd sweet-talk one of her colleagues into showing them to him.

She exerted more pressure on the gas pedal, and ten minutes later she was home. Once inside the lobby, she paused to text Brad that she'd arrived safe and sound, then continued toward her unit.

His response was immediate—a thumbs-up next to her text, followed by a brief message of his own.

Thank you again for being there today. It helped more than you'll ever know. Talk to you soon.

She sighed.

They would indeed talk soon.

But it wasn't going to be a happy conversation.

She dug out her key, opened her door, and tossed her purse on the hall table before continuing toward the bedroom. Since she was too wired to sleep, may as well check voicemails.

As she perched on the side of the bed, she scanned the ones that had come in since she'd put her phone on silent. She could listen to all of them tomorrow—except the one from Jamie that had been left at ten o'clock. That needed immediate attention.

Pulse picking up, she played back the message.

"Hi, Sam. It's Jamie." The young woman's voice was so shaky her words were hard to understand. "You said I could call anytime. I hope this isn't too late. Listen, when you get this could you call me back? It doesn't matter what time. I'll be up. Thanks."

Dread pooled in Sam's stomach.

Like earlier in the church with Brad, bad vibes were wafting her way.

But delaying the call wasn't going to change whatever Jamie had to say.

She forced herself to take several long, slow breaths and placed the call.

Two rings in, Jamie answered. "Sam?"

"Yes. I'm sorry it took me so long to get back to you. I was with a friend who was dealing with a crisis and had my phone on silent. What's going on?"

"I caved."

Sam closed her eyes.

That had always been a possibility, but after their last session she'd thought Jamie was leaning the other way.

"Tell me about it." She tried for a caring, empathetic, non-judgmental tone. Because after making a decision like that, Jamie was going to need all the understanding she could get. Now, and in the years to come.

"They all ganged up on me. John threatened to dump me if I had the baby, and Mom and Dad said they wouldn't pay my college tuition because I didn't have time to be a mother and a student. I brought up the idea of adoption, but they were all against that. Mom said it would be crazy to put my body through nine months of stress because some stranger wanted a baby. And she said going through with the pregnancy would humiliate her and D-Dad."

So pressure had been brought to bear.

Not uncommon, but always unconscionable.

Sam fisted her hand, which still bore the sting marks that continued to smart.

But Jamie's news hurt far worse.

She swallowed. "Tell me how you're feeling about all this."

As the young woman poured out her heart, Sam listened—and wondered, as she always did in these cases, if there was something else she could have done or said or offered that would have made a difference.

But at this point, all she could do was listen…and pray for the eighteen-year-old on the other end of the line. Because the days and weeks and months and years ahead weren't going to be easy for a woman like Jamie, who'd had serious moral concerns that would come back to haunt her.

"So in the end, I did what everyone thought I should do. But it still feels wrong."

And it always would.

But Sam left that unsaid as Jamie concluded. She'd learn the truth of that on her own.

"Right now you need to take care of yourself. How are you doing physically?"

"Okay. Mom took me to a professional place."

"Still, give your body a few days to recover. And I'll be here if you want to talk again."

"Thank you. And I'm sorry I didn't have the strength to see this through." Her voice was laced with tears.

"You don't have to apologize to me, Jamie. I understand how hard it can be to resist pressure. Try to get some sleep tonight. And if you have a relationship with God, prayer might be helpful." Not a suggestion she'd ever offered to a client before, but after weeks of Bible class she was beginning to appreciate the power of prayer.

"I might try that. Good night, Sam. And thanks for listening."

When the call ended, Sam followed the advice she'd given Jamie. She spoke to God, asking the Almighty to watch over the young woman who'd made such a heart-rending choice.

Because while ending the life of an innocent child often took only minutes, it exacted a price that lasted a lifetime.

As she knew all too well.

* * *

"I'd say our seventieth birthday shindig for Dad is a smashing success."

As Rebecca spoke behind him, Brad angled toward her from the spot he'd claimed on the sidelines that offered him a view of the dance floor, where Dad and Sam were doing an enthusiastic swing. "Agreed. Dad seems to be having a great time."

"So does Sam. You, not so much. What gives?"

Leave it to his sister to pick up his unsettled mood. Her instincts were even better now than they'd been when she was younger.

And there was no reason to be reticent about his feelings for Sam—or his frustration about his lack of progress on that front.

"I'm not sure where I stand with Sam. She's been avoiding me for most of the party. And a few days ago she sent a colleague to show me a house I asked to see instead of coming herself." He propped a shoulder against the wall and folded his arms. "I'm beginning to think she's losing interest."

"She's not."

He turned toward his sister. "How do you know?"

"I've been watching her. She's been keeping tabs on you all afternoon. And the look in her eyes can only be described as smitten."

He glanced back at Sam. "I'm not seeing that."

"She masks it whenever you look at her."

"Then why does she seem to be backing off—or at the very least keeping me at arm's length?"

An odd expression flitted across Rebecca's face, come and gone so fast it was possible he'd imagined it. "People can have reasons for keeping their distance. Why don't you just ask her about it?"

"I've been trying not to spook her. Push her to reveal more than she's ready to share. But since she seems to be slipping away despite that, I may take your advice."

The song ended, and after giving his father a hug Sam returned to her table and picked up her purse.

"I think she's leaving." Rebecca nodded toward her.

A few seconds later his sister's speculation proved accurate when Sam wove toward them through the tables, her smile a tad too bright.

"Rebecca, it was a wonderful lunch. You and Brad did a great job on the party. Your dad is having a blast." Sam spared him no more than a quick glance as she spoke.

"I'm glad you enjoyed it. Dad was thrilled you could come. And now, if you'll both excuse me, I have to do a few things in the kitchen. That's the downside of hosting a family birthday party in your place of business." Rebecca shot him a quick glance, and he telegraphed her a silent 'thank you' for setting him and Sam up for a few moments alone together.

"You've been the life of the party." He gave Sam his full attention.

"That's me. The party girl." Her smile didn't waver, but the light in her eyes dimmed a few watts. "Always good for a few laughs."

This was the sassy, brassy Sam he'd first met. The one Laura had aways described.

But it wasn't the one he'd come to know.

Their kiss must have freaked her out big-time if she was running so scared she had to retreat behind her vampy image.

And it was time to find out why.

"I don't see you that way."

At his quiet comment, her smile faded. "It would be better for you if you did. That kind of woman would be totally unsuitable for a minister."

"We need to talk about that."

She took a shaky breath. "Yes, we do. But not here. My schedule is packed the next couple of days, but I'll text you and we can set up a time later in the week."

"Is that a promise?"

"Yes."

Waiting would be hard, but this wasn't the time or place for the kind of conversation he wanted to have anyway. "Let me walk you to your car."

"No." She took a step back. "It's the middle of the day and we're in a small town. I'm fine. And I'd rather save any more conversation for later in the week."

Negative vibes wafted his way—and suddenly he was fine with waiting a few days for what could be bad news. "Okay. If I don't hear from you, you'll hear from me."

"I said I'd text, and I keep my promises. Enjoy this time with your dad. He's a great guy."

And then she was gone, winding through the tables and disappearing out the door.

Leaving him with the same lost, hopeless feeling he'd experienced in church the day of the suicide.

Except there was still hope for this situation. No one had died.

And he wasn't going to give up on Sam without a fight.

* * *

No, no, no, no, no!

Sam jammed the brake to the floor, tires squealing as a child's bike darted in front of her through the deepening dusk. Jerked the steering wheel, her tires squealing on the pavement.

But the dull thud against the bumper told her she'd applied them too late.

Everything after that seemed to happen in slow motion.

The car glided across the wet pavement. Slid off the road and onto the shoulder. Nosedived into a ditch. Slammed into a telephone pole.

Her temple banged against the window on the door, and waves of blackness swept over her.

And then there was nothing.

Until a distorted face peered down at her, moving in and out of focus. Though the woman's features were fuzzy, her words were clear as she shouted the same message over and over and over.

"You killed my baby! You killed my baby! You killed—"

Sucking in a sharp breath, Sam jolted awake and sat bolt upright in bed, chest heaving, heart racing, lungs balking.

The familiar nightmare that used to disrupt her sleep on a regular basis was back.

And it didn't take a genius to figure out why.

Tomorrow morning she was going to tell Brad her story, leaving out none of the gory details. And after she did, there was a strong probability she wouldn't even have to be the one to break things off. It was possible he'd do it for her.

Because if she hadn't been able to forgive herself for seventeen long years, how could she expect him to overlook her culpability in the death of that innocent child? He wouldn't even want to be friends with a woman like her, let alone anything more.

She forced herself to take long, deep breaths until her pulse slowed and her lungs kicked back in. Then she sank back against the headboard and pulled the sheet up to her chin, vision misting.

If only she could erase that terrible trauma. Change the tragic outcome.

But history couldn't be rewritten. As her parents had always said, if you made your bed you had to lie in it.

Choking back a sob, she picked up her phone from the nightstand and squinted at the time on the screen.

Four-fifteen.

No way was she going to be able to go back to sleep. Not after that nightmare—and the looming conversation with Brad that would be the finale for her one brief taste of romance with the finest man she'd ever met.

Heaving a sigh, she swung her legs to the floor. Stood. May as well start her day early. She had plenty of work to do.

Not that she got much done, though, as night gave way to day. It was impossible to concentrate on paperwork, and too easy to make mistakes on big-dollar house deals.

So in the end, she passed the time by perusing new listings, driving by a few that caught her eye for clients in house-hunting mode, and stopping at her favorite coffee shop for a caffeine infusion.

Six hours later, when Brad pulled up in front of the contemporary ranch house that had just listed yesterday and met all his criteria, she was as ready as she'd ever be to break the news.

Meaning she wasn't ready at all.

But this was what she had to do.

He raised a hand in greeting as he slid from behind the wheel, but his smile of greeting flattened as he drew close.

No surprise.

Though she'd applied her makeup with a heavy hand, there was no disguising the half-moon shadows beneath her lashes, the faint fan of lines radiating from the corners of her eyes, the taut skin over her cheekbones, or her pasty complexion.

Alarm flared in his eyes as he stopped beside her on the porch. Touched her arm. "Are you okay?"

She forced up the corners of her mouth. "Bad night. But good news for you on the house front. I think I found your dream home. It checks all your boxes. I took a quick look late yesterday even though it's not officially listed yet and I knew I needed to get you in ASAP."

"I appreciate that, but you don't look up to a house showing."

"I've never let a rough night interfere with my job." She swiveled away, keyed in the access code for the lockbox, and opened the door with the key she retrieved. "Let's do a walk-through, and then we'll talk." About more than the house.

Drawing on every ounce of her willpower, she kept business front and center for the next forty-five minutes as they poked through every corner of the house and the yard. Brad played along, despite the worried looks he kept sending her way.

When they wrapped up under the vaulted ceiling in the living room, she turned to him. "So what do you think?"

"What do *you* think?"

"The truth? I love it. If I were in the market for a house, I'd buy it. It's modern, but not too stark. And it's bright and airy and spacious. I know the price is a little more than you wanted to spend, but I think it's worth the investment. This is a solid neighborhood, and values have steadily risen here. It's also close to your church, so there's a convenience factor. But in the end, you have to live here, so it has to be a place you'd enjoy coming home to."

"It is. You nailed exactly what I wanted." He propped his fists on his hips and gave the living room another scan. "Let's make an offer. What would be reasonable?"

Once they decided on an amount, she took a deep breath and motioned toward the front of the house. "Now that our business is done, can we sit for a few minutes? There are some things I need to say."

"Likewise."

"There's a park across the street. I scoped it out earlier. Is that okay?"

He scrutinized her, his expression somber. "Sure."

They exited the house, and after she locked up she led the way to the small neighborhood park that was empty at this hour of the morning except for a mother and toddler at the far end, by the playground.

She led him toward the secluded bench she'd spotted earlier, sat, and knitted her fingers together in her lap as she tried to fill her uncooperative lungs with air. "First of all, I need to apologize. I let our friendship edge into romance, and I should have backed off before that happened."

His brow crinkled "Why?"

"Because I don't plan to marry again, and I think you may have serious intentions."

The furrows on his forehead deepened. "My intentions *are* serious. But why don't you want to marry again?"

She swallowed.

Might as well just lay the hard truth on the table right up front.

"Because I don't deserve a happy ending."

11

In the silence that followed Sam's startling declaration, Brad tried to regroup.

He'd thought of a lot of reasons she might have decided to back off. Like her previous bad experience with marriage. Their polar-opposite backgrounds. A concern that she wasn't suitable to be a minister's wife. Worries that she fell short compared to Rachel. Some indiscretions in her past with other men, perhaps. And he'd come prepared to address all of those.

But not believing she deserved a happy ending?

That hadn't even been on his radar.

Yet given the abject misery in her eyes, whatever had prompted her conclusion wasn't something he could fix with a few platitudes or reassurances. Her stance was long-standing and well-entrenched, and she had reasons she felt were sound for imposing such a harsh sentence on herself.

Addressing this was going to require every ounce of skill he had as a minister—and as a man.

Keeping his posture open, he gentled his voice. "I have a feeling there's an unhappy story behind that statement."

"Yes. It goes back to Randy."

That didn't compute. Based on the little he knew about her short-lived marriage, her husband had done *her* wrong.

Did she somehow think it was *her* fault that her ex had left her?

"Okay." He rested his elbow on the back of the bench and angled more toward her. "Tell me what happened."

She drew a shaky breath. "I got pregnant only two months after we married. He wasn't happy. He…he told me if I didn't get rid of the baby he'd leave me."

At that bombshell, and the implications, his stomach clenched.

Because as far as he knew, Sam had never had a child.

This story was taking a turn he hadn't expected.

"How did you handle that?" He kept his voice as neutral as possible.

"Not well." Her throat worked, and she rubbed her forehead. "I panicked. I didn't know what to do. I didn't really want a child at that point in my life, either. And I didn't want to lose Randy. I was estranged from my parents, and I had no one else to turn to. I didn't have a job or any money, and without Randy I wouldn't even have had a place to live."

"That was a hard position to be in." He managed to sound empathetic despite the roiling in his stomach.

"Yeah, it was. But despite Randy's threats, and even though I got more and more scared and desperate, I couldn't bring myself to end the life growing inside me. Yet there didn't seem to be any other option. Between the strain and the pregnancy, I was exhausted." She drew a shuddering breath.

When the silence between them stretched, Brad fisted his hands and gave voice to the obvious conclusion. "Did you have an abortion?"

Her head jerked toward him, and she frowned. As if his question surprised her. "No. I told you, I couldn't do that."

This wasn't making sense.

"Are you saying you had the baby?"

155

"No." She sniffed. Wiped the back of her hand under her nose. "This is where the story gets really bad."

As far as he was concerned, it was bad enough already.

But clearly the worst was yet to come.

He braced as Sam picked up her story.

"One night, as Randy was getting ready to go to a band job, he laid down an ultimatum. It was him or the baby, and I had three days to make a decision. After he left, I lay down on the bed in the motel room he'd rented for the gig. I wanted to escape to the oblivion of sleep, but even though I was beyond tired I couldn't doze off. Then I thought about the pills Randy took. The uppers and downers. He never had any trouble sleeping when he took the downers, and I figured it couldn't hurt to take one or two."

But it had.

He knew that deep in his gut.

"Did you have a bad reaction?"

"I had an *over*reaction. Because I took the wrong one. Instead of getting sleepy, I got hyper. My heart started pounding and energy was pumping through me. All I could think to do was get fresh air and wait for the effects to pass. The drummer for the band had picked up Randy, so I decided to take a drive in the rain. Roll down the window and let the air rush into my face."

Brad did the tragic math. Drugs plus car plus rain equaled bad news. "Was there an accident?"

"Yes." A tear brimmed on her lower lashes. Trickled down her cheek. "I drove for almost two hours, until I started to feel more normal. At that point I decided to go back to the motel. I was on the outskirts of town when...when a child on a bike darted into my p-path."

As Sam described the accident—and her encounter with the

child's mother in the ER—her voice grew choppier.

And when she finished with a twist he hadn't seen coming, his stomach coiled into a tight knot.

"I had abdominal injuries, and after surgery the doctor came to see me. He said I'd not only lost my baby, but that I might never be able to conceive again." She dipped her head, and when she spoke again pain was etched in every whispered word. "You know what Randy said when he found out? That I could have found an easier way to take care of the problem, but at least it was over."

Brad mashed his lips together as anger coursed through him.

In her moment of greatest trauma, that's what her husband had said to her?

What a colossal…jerk was too mild a word, but as a minister that was about as brutal as he could get without venturing into very unChristian language.

And Randy had been wrong. Nothing had been over. For seventeen years, Sam had punished herself for what had happened on that rainy night. She was atoning for what she felt had been a grievous mistake that had claimed two lives.

That's why she didn't think she deserved a happy ending.

And despite her husband's cavalier comment that the problem was gone, he'd left her anyway to fend for herself.

Brain reeling, he reached for her icy hand. "I'm so sorry, Sam."

"Me too." Her voice hiccupped. "There were days I wish I'd n-never regained consciousness after the accident. There still are. But I've learned to carry on despite the g-guilt."

He should offer some words of comfort, as he would if a congregant came to him with a confession like this, but none came to mind.

Because Sam's story had a personal impact on him as well as her. Not only had a multitude of bad decisions led to the death of a young child and an unborn baby, but a union with Sam might be childless.

A hard pill to swallow for a man who'd always wanted a family—even if adoption was a potential option.

"In case you're wondering, I wasn't prosecuted."

At her wobbly follow-up, he took a steadying breath.

His brain was so muddled, the potential legal implication hadn't even occurred to him.

"What did the authorities say?"

"Witnesses in a car going the other direction told the police the collision was unavoidable. That the boy flew out of the bushes with no warning, right into my path. And the blood work they did on me didn't show an illegal level of drugs. But I know my reflexes were compromised that night. And because of my irresponsibility, two innocent lives were ended."

His ministerial skills finally kicked in, and he took her hand even as he continued to process all she'd told him. "It sounds like you're being too harsh on yourself."

"No, I'm not." She eased her fingers from his grasp. Picked up her purse. "I've thought about this for seventeen years, Brad. That little boy would be a grown man now. My baby would be on the cusp of college. Instead, they're both dead. And if they can't have a happy ending, neither should I." She stood and faced him, knuckles white as she squeezed the strap of her purse, her eyes pools of grief and misery. "I'm sorry. For everything." Her voice choked, and she took a step back. "I'll put the offer in for the house and let you know what they say."

He rose too. "Sam, we should talk about—"

"No." She retreated another step. "There's nothing to talk

about. Someday I hope you find a woman to love who will be everything you deserve. But that's not me, as much as I wish it could be."

Another tear trailed down her cheek, and with a choked sob she pivoted and dashed toward her car.

"Sam!" He started after her. "Wait!"

But she didn't. Instead, she ran faster.

His step slowed.

He couldn't make her stay and talk to him. And in her present state, it wasn't likely she'd be receptive to anything he had to say anyway—whatever that might be. He had no idea at this point.

All he knew for sure was that nothing she'd said changed how he felt about her.

Convincing her of that, however, could be a challenge.

And until he came up with a plan of action and they both calmed down, it might be best to send some messages of support and caring—but keep his distance.

* * *

Today had gone just about as well—or as badly—as she'd expected.

Sam tugged another tissue from the box on her bed, blew her nose, and continued to throw clothes into her suitcase.

Maybe leaving town for a week was foolish. And her boss hadn't been thrilled by the impromptu vacation request. But once she'd assured him she'd keep her finger on business from afar and that she'd line up other agents to handle pending transactions and showings, he'd been more amenable. After all, she rarely took time off, and how could he argue when she'd said she had emergency personal business to attend to?

Which hadn't been a lie.

Tending to a broken heart qualified as both an emergency and personal business.

She tossed her toiletries bag into the suitcase and zipped it shut.

Now all she had to do was text Laura.

She pulled out her cell and typed in a brief message.

> Have to cancel lunch tomorrow. Sorry. Taking an unexpected trip to Chicago for a few days. Talk to you when I get back.

Less than thirty seconds later, animated dots indicated her best friend was responding.

> What's up? Everything okay?

> Fine. Have some business to attend to.

> Are you selling real estate up there now too?

> No. This is personal business.

No activity on the screen.

Good.

If Laura pressed, she'd have to bob and weave, and she wasn't in the mood to—

Her cell began to ring, and Laura's name appeared on the screen.

Sam weighed the phone in her hand.

She could let the call roll to voicemail, but Laura would

know she was being ignored because they'd just been texting.

Not an option.

Calling up her cheeriest voice, she accepted the call. "Hi, kiddo. Sorry to cancel on you, but look on the bright side. You'll have an extra couple of hours this weekend with that handsome groom of yours."

"He won't object. But I've been looking forward to our lunch. Listen—are you sure everything's okay? You never take unplanned trips."

"Well, there's a first for everything, right? I've been working too many long hours and the pace finally caught up with me. I need a few days of R&R."

"Will you be back for Bible class on Thursday?"

"That's my plan."

"How about your Tuesday night commitment?"

"No. I'm skipping that this week." No way could she counsel troubled young women when she was a basket case herself.

"Is there anything I can do for you while you're gone?"

"No. The garden will be fine for a few days. I'll water everything before I leave."

A few beats ticked by.

"There's something you're not telling me, isn't there?"

Of course her intuitive best friend would pick up bad vibes. Laura was wired that way.

"Everything will be fine, Laura. Trust me."

"Is it okay if I say a few prayers for you?"

"Prayers are always welcome. Gotta run, kiddo."

Once they said their goodbyes, Sam typed in a text for Brad. One she'd send after she was on the road, just in case he had any inclination to try to stop her.

But that was unlikely, given the shock on his face when she'd

161

left him at the park a couple of hours ago after her download. Considering all she'd laid on him, it was no wonder he'd been reeling.

By now, though, he'd no doubt realized that her decision to walk away was the best thing that could have happened. That he'd dodged a bullet.

And someday—maybe—the emptiness in her heart would be less painful.

But in the meantime she could use all the prayers Laura sent her way.

12

He needed information.

And who better than Sam's best friend to provide it?

The instant he finished his first service on Sunday, Brad changed out of his clerical vestments and headed for the fellowship hall. Laura and Nick usually stayed for coffee, but if she wasn't there he'd call her.

Because from everything he knew about her, Sam was acting peculiar.

And that was more than alarming.

When he entered the hall, he stayed off to the side and scanned the room. The instant he spotted Laura, he motioned to her, then stepped back outside before any of the congregants could corner him. Not his usual pattern during the social hour, but this wasn't a usual situation.

When she joined him, she frowned. "What's up?"

"I need to talk to you. In private. The small meeting room is free." He strode ahead, then stepped aside when they reached it so she could enter. As soon as she was inside, he followed and closed the door halfway.

Laura cocked her head and scrutinized him. "Are you okay? I thought you looked a little under the weather during your sermon, but it's more noticeable up close."

"I could be better. Do you know where Sam is?"

A flicker of understanding dawned in her eyes. "Ah. So this is about Sam."

"Yes." He wasn't going to pretend with his childhood friend. "I got one text from her late Friday afternoon, saying she was going to be out of town and that she'd shuffled me off to a colleague to do the paperwork for the house I'm planning to buy. She hasn't responded to any of my texts since then, and she's letting my calls roll to voicemail."

"Did you two have a fight?"

"No. We had a...discussion. She shared some information that I probably didn't respond to as well as I should have."

Scratch probably.

He'd blown it big-time.

What Sam had needed was understanding and love and acceptance and a hug and a dozen other things he should have provided. *Would* have provided if he hadn't been so blindsided by her rapid-fire string of revelations.

Laura folded her arms. "You know, despite the Teflon veneer she presents to the world, Sam's feelings run deep. She's much more easily hurt than she lets on." There was a hint of censure in her tone.

And it was deserved.

"I know. And I have amends to make. Do you know where she is?"

Laura considered him for a moment before she responded. "Chicago. But I don't know where she's staying."

"Do you know when she'll be back?"

"Not in time for her counseling center work on Tuesday night, but she said she'd be here for Bible study on Thursday."

He stared at her.

Counseling center?

Bible study?

Eyes widening, Laura clapped a hand over her mouth. "Oh, shoot. I wasn't supposed to say anything about Bible study."

"Too late. Now that you've spilled it, I need details."

Laura shifted her weight from one foot to the other, forehead pinching. "Sam's been going with me to Bible study for months."

Brad clenched his fingers.

All these weeks, while he'd been wrestling with the notion of getting involved with someone who didn't practice her faith, she'd been going to Bible study. No doubt learning all about mercy and forgiveness and love—the very principles he'd neglected to demonstrate on Friday.

"Tell me about her counseling center work." His voice sounded hollow even to his own ears.

Laura propped a hip on the conference room table and folded her arms. "I guess I can do that. She didn't ask me to keep *that* a secret, and she's been doing it forever. The center works with young unmarried pregnant girls and women, giving them any support they need to carry their babies to full term. Sam told me someone recruited her years ago, and she stuck with it because it was worthwhile work. It wasn't the sort of volunteer gig I'd have expected her to gravitate toward, but with her down-to-earth, tell-it-like-it-is manner, I expect it's a good fit."

Better than Laura could ever guess, if Sam had never shared her full history with her best friend.

And it wasn't hard to figure out Sam's rationale for that volunteer gig. She couldn't restore life to the children who'd died the night of the accident, but she could help other young women who found themselves in her situation. Let them know they weren't alone, that someone cared, that they had options.

Perhaps that was her way of atoning for the sins she thought she bore.

"Hey." Laura touched his arm, her voice quiet. "Do you remember the sermon you gave last Christmas Eve? About mending relationships and saying 'I'm sorry'? It gave me new hope when I needed it most. And those two words *do* make a difference. Maybe you just need to follow your own advice."

Maybe he did.

The sooner the better.

"Thanks for the counsel—and for listening."

"Call me if I can do anything to help."

"I will."

She squeezed his arm and slipped through the door.

As quiet descended, he filled his lungs.

He ought to pop in to the social hour, like he always did. But he wasn't in the mood to smile and schmooze today.

Instead, he returned to the church and sank down on one of the pews in the back corner for some serious soul-searching.

And one fact took center stage at once.

Despite the shocking story she'd relayed on Friday, he still loved Sam. He knew that as surely as he knew the sun would rise tomorrow.

He also knew that the woman who'd claimed his heart would never, ever purposely hurt anyone.

Seventeen years ago she'd been a frightened teenager, driven by deep despair and desperation, coping as best she knew how. Yes, she'd made mistakes. And she'd paid for those mistakes every day of her life since, shouldering the blame for the tragic accident that had taken two lives.

Maybe her reflexes had been impaired, as she'd claimed, even if there'd been no legal grounds to charge her with a crime. Yet judgment was God's prerogative, not his. And God offered forgiveness and a second chance to those who repented, as she clearly had.

As for the possibility that a union with Sam might be child-less—there was never any guarantee on that score anyway, even with couples who had no obvious impediments to conceiving. And there were plenty of children who needed a home if he and Sam couldn't have their own biological child.

Bottom line, he could live with everything Sam had told him.

What he couldn't live without was *her*. She was so much a part of his life now it was impossible to imagine a future that didn't include her.

The challenge was how to convince a woman who felt unworthy of love or happiness, who'd resigned herself to a solitary existence as a penance for her mistakes, that forgiveness wasn't just a theory preached in the pulpit. That mercy and understanding and absolution were real, and that they applied to her. On both the human and divine level.

His stomach clenched.

He'd done a terrible job of that on Friday. No matter the muddle he'd been in after her shocking revelations, letting her walk away had been a huge mistake. She hadn't needed time to calm down. She'd needed to be told she was loved—by him and by God.

Bowing his head, he opened his heart to the Almighty—and prayed for guidance.

And by the time he rose half an hour later to vest for the second service, he had a plan.

* * *

"Laura! Wait!" Sam grabbed her best friend's arm as she headed toward the front of the room at Bible study.

Laura turned. "What's wrong?"

"Let's sit in the back." Like usual.

"I can't. I agreed to be the facilitator for one of the discussion groups next week, and Jenna saved us seats so she could fill me in on the protocol before we start tonight."

Sam waved a hand toward the last row. "I think I'll sit back there."

"Oh, come on. It won't kill you to sit in front this once. It's not like in school, where you could be called on to participate even if you didn't want to."

Sam blew out a breath. After her anything-but-restful trip to Chicago, she was too tired to argue. "Fine."

They claimed two seats, and while Laura conferred with Jenna, Sam slumped in her chair and tried without much success to chill out.

When the leader of the group at last stepped up to the podium, the room grew silent. "Good evening, everyone. As you know, our guest speaker this evening was going to lead off tonight's session, but he had to cancel. However, we have a substitute, and I'm sure his talk will provide us with plenty of ideas for our discussion groups. Please welcome Reverend Brad Matthews."

What?

Sam's back stiffened and she lurched upright.

As Brad entered the room from a side door and moved to the podium, she shot Laura a suspicious look. Leaned closer. "You knew about this, didn't you?"

"No. I didn't know he was coming. He just emailed and asked me to make sure *you* came."

"And you didn't ask why?"

"I didn't want to get in the middle of whatever is going on between you two. But for the record, sitting in the front row was my idea."

So Laura was subtly complicit in whatever plan Brad had concocted.

Some friend *she'd* turned out to be.

Sam eyed the exit door—but bolting wasn't an option. Leaving now would draw too much attention to her. Besides, she and Laura had driven here together, and Laura was the chauffeur tonight.

She was stuck.

"Sam." Laura touched her arm, and she looked back. "I'm sorry if what I did was out of line. I just want what's best for you."

At her friend's contrite demeanor, Sam let out a slow breath.

Laura was the best friend she'd ever had, and it was hard to fault someone whose intentions were good.

She forced up the corners of her mouth. "Don't worry, kiddo. I know you meant well."

As Brad took his place behind the podium, she gave him a surreptitious once-over.

He always radiated a strength and integrity that inspired confidence and trust, especially when attired in clerical garb. But tonight the lines at the corners of his eyes and the shadows underneath spoke of sleepless nights and worry.

Last Friday's conversation must have taken a heavy toll on him too.

And that was her fault.

She should have listened to her instincts from the get-go, acknowledged he was getting serious, and backed off far sooner.

But even though he'd shown up tonight, suggesting he wasn't ready to give up on them, in time he'd realize he was better off without her.

Or had he already moved on?

Because other than a brief glance in her direction when he entered, he didn't give her any special attention. Nor did he make eye contact again.

So why was he here tonight?

Whatever his reason, his talk on forgiveness dovetailed with the book of Ephesians they were focusing on in this session. The message in Paul's letter was uplifting, but as she'd discovered, while the notion of forgiveness was heartening in theory, practical applications were another matter.

As Brad neared the end of his talk, Sam began to plot her escape.

She couldn't leave without Laura, but she could flee to the ladies' room and hide out there until Brad was gone. He couldn't hang around forever.

Maybe that was the coward's way out, but she wasn't ready to face him yet.

When she started to lean over to tell Laura her plan, Brad closed his notes and looked directly at her.

She froze as he spoke.

"I know the focus of your study is Ephesians, and forgiveness is a prominent theme in that book. But it also receives a great deal of attention elsewhere in scripture. Matthew tells us not to judge, so that we may not be judged. And he tells us we must forgive not seven times, but seventy times seven. In Ezekiel we read about the new life that comes to those who repent and do what is right and just. The message is clear. Our God is a God of mercy, who's always ready to offer forgiveness and a second chance. And if God does that for us, how can we do any less for each other—and for ourselves?"

He picked up his notes, never breaking eye contact with her. "Forgiveness isn't always easy to practice, especially when someone you love fails you or hurts you. But as Paul reminds us in Ephesians, we should be kind and merciful to one another, forgiving each other as God forgives us. If someone wasn't there when you needed them…if they failed to demonstrate their love…give them a chance to say they're sorry. Because broken relationships *can* be mended. All it takes is forgiveness given in love. And love is the key. Because as the Bible tells us, love never fails."

As the group gave Brad a round of applause, Sam tried to fill her lungs.

His beautiful words of healing, spoken from the heart, had been meant for her.

And she couldn't argue with the content of his message. She'd been in Bible study long enough to know that the message of forgiveness was prominent in scripture.

As for repentance, she couldn't be sorrier for all the mistakes she'd made.

So was it possible she could give them to God, let them go, and at last move on?

And was it also possible Brad loved her despite all the mistakes she'd made?

Somehow that seemed too much to hope for.

Yet at the warmth and reassurance in his eyes, a tiny ember of hope stirred to life among the cold ashes in her heart.

The leader stepped forward to thank Brad, and as the Bible group members rose to reconvene in small discussion groups Laura leaned over and spoke in a low voice. "If you decide to cut out early tonight, feel free. We'll catch up later." She nodded toward Brad, who'd extricated himself from the leader and was moving her way.

Sam watched him approach, her heart playing a frenzied game of hopscotch.

When he reached her, he angled away from the group and lowered his voice. "In case there's any doubt, my concluding comments were for you." His voice was husky as he searched her face. "Since you wouldn't respond to any of my messages, I decided I'd have to go the captive-audience route. But I'd like to continue this discussion in private, if you're willing."

"Okay." It was all she could manage.

She fell in beside him as they left the church hall, and once they were outside he took her hand while they walked toward his car, his grasp strong yet tender, comforting but also thrilling.

Not until she was in the passenger seat and he was behind the wheel did he speak again. "Let me cut to the chase, Sam. I'm sorrier than I can ever express for letting you walk out of that park last Friday. My only excuse, flimsy though it may be, is that my mind was on overload. At the time, I had a misguided sense that we both needed space. But that was a bad call. I think what we needed was this."

Slowly, never breaking eye contact, he reached over. Cupped her cheek with his palm. Stroked his thumb over her skin with a feather-soft touch that left fire in its wake.

Her eyelids fluttered closed as hope and anticipation bubbled up inside her like the effervescence in a glass of champagne.

But no alcoholic beverage would ever produce an effect this potent.

"I'd like to kiss you, Sam." Brad's voice rasped, and she opened her eyes to find him watching her with a hunger and a longing that sent a rush of warmth through her.

"I…I don't really know how to kiss a minister."

One side of his mouth quirked up, but the intensity in his irises didn't dim one iota. "I'll tell you what. Just try kissing a man."

Then he leaned toward her, slow but steady, and pressed his lips to hers.

Somewhere very close by, fireworks started going off.

Because this was nothing like the first heady but simple kiss he'd given her. This was an all-in, all-consuming lip-lock fueled by pent-up desire—and it left her breathless and tingling…and wanting more.

When he at last drew back, she had to coax her lungs to kick in again.

"Wow." It was all she could manage. "I didn't know ministers could kiss like that."

His mouth flexed again. "I'm glad it passed muster. To tell you the truth, I was a little intimidated. Except for Rachel, I haven't had a lot of experience at this. I was afraid I might fall short in the romance department."

Because she'd dated a lot more than he had, and he was worried she'd compare him to other guys.

They needed to talk about that, even if she'd rather leave her history in the past and go back for a second helping of what he'd just dished up.

But if the two of them were going to get serious, there were issues that had be addressed—and background that had to be shared. There could be no secrets between them, no problems left undiscussed.

She took a deep breath. "For the record, you kiss better than any guy I've ever dated. And I've kissed more than my share of men. In fact, in the interest of full disclosure, I—"

"Sam." He pressed a gentle fingertip to her lips. "You don't have to bare your soul about the men in your past. All that matters to me is what we have together. I've known you long enough to get a solid sense of the kind of person you are *now*. Whatever happened before isn't relevant."

While his words were a balm to her soul, she wanted this relationship to be built on full transparency.

"I appreciate that, but I want you to know what you're getting with me."

He studied her for a moment, then nodded. "If you want to tell me about your past, I'm fine with that. I just want you to know it's not necessary. And no matter what you share, it won't change how I feel about you."

Hopefully that was true, but going forward she wasn't keeping anything from him—the good, the bad, or the ugly.

"I want you to know that while I wasn't nearly as wild as I have a feeling you think I was when we met, after Randy dumped me my self-esteem was in the toilet. For a year or two I was a hermit. But the loneliness was overwhelming, so eventually I joined a singles group." She swallowed.

This was the part she was ashamed of.

Nevertheless, she took a fortifying breath and pushed on, the words bitter on her tongue. "Twice during those early years the loneliness got so bad that I...I had a one-night stand. I thought that would fill the empty place in my heart, but it didn't. It only made everything worse. So I swore off casual intimacy. That's why I went out with so many men. Most guys expect a payoff, so my dating roster changed often. But even casual dating got old. The truth is, I rarely date at all anymore."

In the silence that followed, she peeked over at him. And the compassion in his expression clogged her throat.

"You want to know what I think?" His voice and demeanor were tender.

Maybe not, but she nodded anyway,

"I think you're a remarkable woman. Strong, resilient, kindhearted, giving. I see someone who's learned from her mistakes and has worked hard to atone for them, and who's seeking to reconnect with God. I see one of the most sensitive, considerate, and caring people I've ever had the privilege to meet. You survived a very difficult period in your life in the only way you knew how at the time. And you emerged a better person. That's the best we can hope for in this imperfect, human world. What matters most to me is that the Sam Reynolds I know is a wonderful, warm woman who has added joy and light and love to my days."

Oh, mercy.

In another minute, she was going to turn into Niagara Falls.

"You're being too kind."

"No, I'm not."

Yes, he was—but she'd save that argument for later. Because there was another hard topic she had to bring forward.

"There's more to consider, Brad. I can't promise you a family. And you'd make a wonderful father."

His gaze held steady. "Since we're being honest here, I'll admit that was one of the things that threw me on Friday. But you know what I realized? I can live without children, if that's God's plan for me. But I can't live without you. That's why I brought this tonight." He reached into the pocket of his jacket and withdrew a small velvet jeweler's box. Set it on the console between them.

Her pulse stuttered as she homed in on the box.

"I know we've only been dating for five months. But as my father and sister told me, that's long enough when you meet the right person. And I have." He took her hand. Wove his fingers through hers. "I love you, Sam. I want to spend the rest of my life waking up next to you, laughing with you, sharing with you, making memories with you. And I want to do it in the house you found for me. Which I got, by the way."

She blinked. Tried to shift gears as she looked up at him. "What?"

"The sellers accepted my bid for the house you showed me on Friday. The colleague who was handling your work for you while you were gone called me right before I came here tonight. I told her to proceed, but I'd rather not live there alone." He picked up the velvet box and flipped it open to reveal a sparkling solitaire. "So here it comes. How would you feel about marrying a minister?"

Her lungs locked as she stared at the ring.

Was this for real, or had she entered a different dimension? One where dreams came true and people really did find happily-ever-afters?

Because in her world, fairy tales only happened in the pages of storybooks.

"Sam? Am I rushing you?" Brad's forehead rumpled. "If you're not ready, I can put this away for now and—"

"No!" She grabbed his hand as he started to retract it. "I just want to make sure you're not rushing things. That you won't have any regrets down the road. I mean, I'm not the domestic type. I can't even cook."

A slow grin bowed his mouth. "Trust me, I know. But I'm used to microwave food. And maybe we can take some cooking classes together. That could be a fun couples activity for newly-weds."

Newlyweds.

What a sweet sound that had.

She scrutinized him. "Are you absolutely sure about this?"

"I couldn't be any more sure. And if you say yes, I'll demon-strate the depth of my conviction." He waggled his eyebrows.

A surge of joy swept through her, so strong it left her dizzy and giddy and speechless.

So she simply held out her left hand.

Brad removed the ring from the case and slipped it on with an endearing unsteadiness. Lifted her hand and kissed each finger before tugging her close, until only the console separated them. "What would you think about a Christmas wedding?"

She smiled and edged closer. "I think that would be the best present I ever got. But I wouldn't object to a sneak peek at what's going to be under the tree, waiting to be unwrapped."

A chuckle rumbled deep in his chest. "I bet you were one of those kids who hated waiting until Christmas morning to open presents and tried to find them ahead of time."

"Guilty as charged. But you, Brad Matthews, are worth waiting for. Especially if you give me a little preview of what to expect on Christmas morning."

"I think that could be arranged." The smoky look in his eyes sent a sizzle through her nerve endings. "But I have an idea that will enhance the preview. Get out of the car."

She peered at him. "What?"

"This console is annoying. Poor planning on my part. Let's relocate to the back seat."

Before she could respond, he opened his door and slid from behind the wheel.

She didn't need a second invitation.

He was already waiting when she climbed in beside him. And he wasted no time pulling her close. "This is much better."

"I haven't necked in the back seat of a car in years." She giggled and snuggled closer.

"I've *never* necked in the back seat of a car. But I don't want to wait to do this, and a minister kissing a woman in full view on a church parking lot could create a scandal. What if someone from Bible study came out? Even in the dark, they might spot us."

"See? I'm a bad influence on you."

"On the contrary. You're an excellent influence—in every way." His eyes softened as he played with a few strands of her hair. "You brought the sunshine back to my world. You filled up the empty place in my heart and refreshed my soul. You made me believe I could have a second chance at love." He released her hair and focused on her lips as his eyes began to smolder. "And now, unless you have something else you want to say, I'm done talking."

She slipped her arms around his neck and smiled up at him. "I'm ready to move from words to action."

"Now you're speaking my language."

He erased the distance between them, and as his lips closed over hers in a tender kiss that spoke more eloquently than words of commitment, caring, and the promise of a future filled with love, Sam finally let go of the past.

Because this was her future.

Here, in Brad's arms, was where she belonged.

For always.

13

"You look beautiful, Sam."

As Laura held out the bouquet of cream-colored roses and holly sprigs, Sam took it, then glanced at her reflection in the bride's-room mirror.

The scalloped hem of her cream-colored sheath ended just above her knees, and the long sleeves were demure. But the neckline—cut straight across, the scalloped edge revealing a glimpse of creamy skin on her shoulders—gave the dress a modest touch of Sam pizzazz, as Laura had called it.

The dress was perfect for a minister's bride.

Her lips curved up. "Not bad, I guess."

Rebecca picked up her bouquet of red roses and holly, which looked spectacular against the forest-green velvet of her bridesmaid dress. "An understatement if I ever heard one. I agree with Laura. You look stunning. And if you have any doubt about that, watch my brother when you walk down the aisle. His jaw is going to drop." She crossed the room and gave her a hug. "I'm going to take my place. The music just changed. And for the record, I couldn't be happier for you and Brad. You two are a perfect couple."

As Brad's sister slipped out the door, Laura's mouth bowed. "She's right, you know."

"I hope so. But it's still hard for me to believe this is real. I would never in a million years have thought I'd end up marrying a minister."

"God works in mysterious ways."

"It would take Agatha Christie to solve *this* mystery. But however it came about, I'll be grateful to the end of my days." Her vision misted, and she sniffed.

"Hey! As you told me on *my* wedding day, no tears or you'll look like a raccoon. You can cry after the pictures."

Sam pulled a tissue from a box on a nearby table and dabbed at her eyes. "You're right, kiddo. That wouldn't be a pretty look."

A soft knock sounded on the door, and Laura crossed the room and twisted the knob.

Henry stuck his head in. "It's starting."

"My cue to exit." Laura came back, gave her a hug, and whispered in her ear. "Love you, Sam."

"Love you back, kiddo." Sam squeezed her, then took a deep breath. "See you in the sanctuary."

As Laura exited, Henry entered. "You sure do look pretty, Sam."

"Thank you. You clean up well too. That tux suits you."

"You think?" He fiddled with the bow tie. "I never wore one before. Brad had to help me with the buttons on the shirt. He said they're called studs, but they're the weirdest buttons I ever saw. They aren't even attached."

Sam's lips quirked. "Well, you look wonderful."

The music changed again, and her pulse picked up. "I think that's our cue, Henry."

"Okay then." He grinned and cocked his elbow. "Let's get this show on the road."

They moved into the vestibule, and when the doors opened they began their slow walk down the aisle of the candlelit church toward the sanctuary, where poinsettias and fir trees adorned in white twinkle lights added a magical glow to the scene.

Sam gave the sea of smiling faces a quick sweep, but her focus was on the man who would soon promise to love her and cherish her all the days of her life.

The man who would soon be her husband.

It was almost surreal.

Yet there he stood, waiting for her, and looking amazing in his tux. Handsome. Distinguished. Stalwart. The latter was an old-fashioned term, but it suited him. Because Brad was honor and steadfastness and fidelity and integrity personified.

And his expression as she approached melted her heart. It was the look every woman wanted to see on the face of the man she loved. Tender, caring, devoted, his features softened by awe and adoration. As if he felt like the luckiest person in the world.

But he wasn't.

That honor belonged to her.

As Henry relinquished his hold and she tucked her arm in Brad's, he smiled down at her and laid a protective hand over hers, his touch steady. Sure. Resolute. His eyes filled with a promise that he would be there for her through good times and bad, in sickness and health, all the days of his life.

In a moment, they'd give voice to those vows before all their friends and family gathered here.

But in her heart, Sam knew that Brad had already made them before God. As had she.

And for all of her days she'd give thanks for the blessing of this special man, who'd taken a chance on a woman who hadn't seemed at all suitable for him—and opened the door to a future filled with love and hope for both of them.

Epilogue

Fourteen months later

Could life be any more perfect?

Lips flexing, Brad took a slow inventory of Sam's features, relaxed and serene in sleep. Then he leaned over, stole a gentle kiss, and backed off to enjoy the show.

She stirred. Burrowed into the pillow. Emitted a small sigh. After a moment, her burnished lashes fluttered against her cheeks. Then her eyelids opened to reveal vivid, if unfocused, green irises. Finally came the smile that warmed her face as her eyes cleared and connected with his. A smile filled with deep, abiding love that always tightened his throat.

As long as he lived, he'd never tire of watching her awaken.

Nor did a day go by that he didn't thank God for sending this remarkable woman into his life.

"Hi, sleepyhead." He brushed a wayward wisp of hair off her forehead. The gray tinge of fatigue that had shaded her face earlier was gone, leaving in its place an almost luminous glow. "How do you feel?"

"Good." The corners of her mouth rose farther north. "And happy. And very grateful."

"Likewise. And also very blessed." He withdrew a single, perfect, long-stemmed rose from behind his back and handed it to her. "Happy Valentine's Day."

"Oh, Brad." She took it. Inhaled the heady, sweet fragrance. "It's beautiful. Thank you."

"There are twenty-three more on the table." He moved aside and motioned to an overflowing vase.

Sam's eyes rounded. "Two dozen roses? Wow. You went all-out. I only got a dozen on our first anniversary."

"That's all you got today too. The second dozen aren't for you."

"They aren't?" She quirked an eyebrow, a teasing light sparking in her eye.

"No." He cocooned her hand between his. "I have to confess...there's another woman in my life now. As of three hours ago. The other dozen are for her."

Sam's lips twitched. "And what might this other woman's name be?"

"Emily." He savored the sound of it on his tongue.

A tender light suffused Sam's face. "And where is Emily?"

Brad reached behind him and lifted a tiny pink bundle. Placed it in Sam's outstretched arms. "Right here. Waiting patiently for her mommy to wake up."

With one finger, Sam touched the tiny but perfect nose, stroked the fuzz of reddish hair, and stared down into their child's trusting, wide blue eyes. "I didn't think I could ever be happier than the day we said I do, but I am." Her voice choked.

As a tear trailed down her cheek, Brad reached over and brushed it away with his fingertip. "No more tears, Sam. Our time for weeping is past. This is our time to laugh—and to love."

"Amen to that." She stroked a finger down Emily's cherubic cheek. "And our circle of love has expanded on the perfect day. That's quite a coincidence."

"Or not. Maybe there was a touch of the divine in this birthday. Because whenever we look at our daughter, we'll be reminded of the miracles love can create."

Her irises began to glisten again, and she lifted her hand. Touched his face. "I'm reminded of that every time I look at you."

"I feel the same." His voice rasped as a tidal wave of emotion swept over him. Hope. Love. Elation. Gratitude. And so much more. A tsunami of feelings that sent his spirits soaring.

Vision misting, he rested one hand on their new daughter and leaned over to claim the lips of the woman who'd brought him joy beyond measure.

But in the moment before her sweet response drove all coherent thought from his mind, he sent a silent prayer of thanks heavenward.

For never in his wildest dreams could he have foreseen this new path his life had taken, nor imagined all the blessings that would grace it.

A beautiful, caring wife to love and to cherish.

A daughter who would fill their days with awe and wonder and delight

And a future as bright and beckoning as the star that had guided three kings to another baby long, long ago.

Life didn't get any better than that.

**Keep reading for a preview of
TILL THERE WAS YOU,
Book 3 in the Circle of Friends series.**

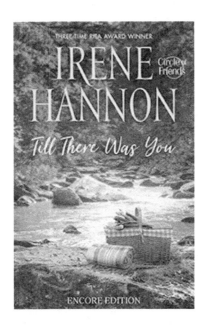

Till There Was You

CIRCLE OF FRIENDS—BOOK 3
ENCORE EDITION

1

"That's a lie!" Anger coursing through him, Zach Wright shot to his feet, planted his hands on the desk that separated him from Ted Larsen, and glared at the managing editor. "A total, complete, absolute lie."

"I'm sure it is." Ted's tone remained calm. "But are you willing to reveal your sources to prove you didn't fabricate the information?"

"You know I can't do that." No journalist worth their salt would commit such a breach of professional ethics.

"Then we have to dial back the heat while we work on a game plan."

"Why? My information is solid. I wouldn't use it if it wasn't."

"I know that. But management is getting serious pressure on this. Including the threat of a lawsuit."

Zach gave a dismissive wave. "That's just a scare tactic."

"Maybe. But it worked—for the moment." Ted rested his

hands one atop the other on his desk. "It's not easy being a lucrative publisher in this day and age, Zach. You know that. Management is being cautious."

He gave a grunt of disgust. "I can think of a less diplomatic word for it."

"Look, we'll work this out. I know your information is sound. We just have to prove it." Ted paused. Linked his fingers. "And until we do, we're going to put the series on ice."

Fury bubbling up inside him, Zach jammed his hands into his pockets, strode over to the window, and stared out at the city streets. St. Louis could be beautiful, but on this dreary February day it was ugly—the same as his mood. This whole experience was leaving a very bad taste in his mouth.

He swung back to Ted. "Whatever happened to printing the truth? I thought that was our job."

"It is. But Simmons's job is to keep the paper solvent. As the publisher, he calls the shots. And he's not willing to risk a lawsuit."

"So we just let them get away with it?" He fisted his hands. "The corruption in that office is rampant—misuse of public funds, a rigged bidding process based on nepotism instead of price, blatant bribery—what am I supposed to do, forget about it?"

"No. Just lie low for a while. In fact, why don't you take some time off? How many weeks of PTO have you accumulated, anyway? Five, six?"

"Eight."

"When was your last real vacation?"

"I don't know." Zach shrugged, making no attempt to mask his impatience. "It's been a while." Like three or four years.

"Maybe you're due."

Now? While he was digging into a hot story that got hotter every day?

What kind of journalist did that?

"I don't want to take a vacation in the middle of this coverage." He squared his shoulders. "The story needs to be told, and I'm not running away from it. I'll stand behind my coverage even if the paper won't."

"We're not asking you to run away. Just hit pause. If you don't want to take a vacation while we figure out how to deal with the allegations, we can assign you to another story."

"Like what?"

"The weather folks are predicting that the Ste. Genevieve area is going to get hit with another flood. I need somebody down there to cover it."

Zach's jaw dropped.

Seriously?

They wanted to assign one of the paper's top investigative reporters to a *weather* story?

He gritted his teeth. "You're kidding, right?"

Ted adjusted his glasses, and at the sudden glint of steel in his eyes a red alert began beeping in Zach's mind.

Maybe he'd overstepped.

After all, Ted was his boss. And his usual affable, easygoing manner could be deceptive. Underneath, he was still the tough-as-nails reporter who'd come up through the ranks and who didn't put up with insubordination.

"No, Zach, I'm not." His tone was edged with iron. "You're overreacting to this situation, whether you realize it or not. You need some time to decompress. Nobody can maintain the intensity, keep up the pace you set, month after month, year after year, without wearing down. A change of scene, a different focus, a fresh perspective could be helpful. You can get that by taking the flood coverage assignment—or by taking a vacation. It's your choice. But those are the only options."

* * *

"In one mile, take Exit 154 toward Ste. Genevieve."

As the voice on his phone spoke, Zach frowned and reduced his speed yet again. With the dense fog, it would be easy to miss the exit ramp and any signs pointing toward it.

He tugged at the knot of silk constricting his throat and drew in a relieved breath as the fabric gave way. Ties were torture devices. But dinner with the publisher was definitely a tie occasion.

At least Simmons had had the guts to discuss the situation with him face-to-face. But even though the publisher had assured him the paper stood behind him and had confidence in his reporting, they'd still hit pause on the series.

As far as Zach was concerned, actions spoke louder than words.

He flexed his taut shoulders and glanced at his watch. Sighed.

Ten o'clock.

It had been a long day. A very long day. And the only upbeat moment had been Ted's parting words.

He played them back in his mind.

"These setbacks happen to all of us, Zach. Don't let it get you down. You're a good reporter. One of the best. We'll work this out."

Satisfying, since Ted's compliments were rare.

In fact…that had been the most satisfying moment in his career for a long time.

Which felt wrong.

Zach frowned and flexed his fingers on the wheel.

His satisfaction used to come from his work. From the feeling he was making a difference.

And that's where it *should* come from. Not from recognition by his boss.

Could that be the source of the discontent, the restlessness, that had plagued him for the past few months?

"Use the right lane and take the next exit."

Zach edged over, squinting as his headlights tried to penetrate the dense fog that was obscuring the lane lines.

In hindsight, given how late the dinner had ended, he should have waited until morning to make this drive.

But that wasn't how he was wired.

He might not be happy about this flood coverage assignment, but doing things halfway wasn't in his DNA. And getting settled in tonight would allow him to dive into the coverage first thing tomorrow.

The sign for Ste. Genevieve loomed out of the mist to his right, and he slowed. Edged onto the ramp when the road veered to the right. Crept along until he hit an intersection. Followed the voice prompt on his phone and turned left.

Man.

This pea soup would do San Francisco proud.

As he inched along the two-lane road toward the French settlement town that was his destination, the shroud of fog insulating him from his surroundings bordered on disorienting. And weird. It was almost like one of those old "Twilight Zone" episodes, and he was the last living creature on earth.

He flicked a gaze to the rearview mirror.

Nothing but fog. No cars, no sign of life.

191

A shiver rippled through him.

He might not be alone in the world, but he was certainly alone on this ghostly road.

Or maybe not quite as alone as he'd thought.

Because when he redirected his attention to the pavement in front of him, a deer materialized from the mist and bolted into his path.

Uttering a word he rarely used, he jerked the wheel hard to the right, heart stuttering.

The deer bounded off—but as his compact car fishtailed across the unforgiving moisture-slicked asphalt, it seemed to have a mind of its own. Despite his attempt to regain control, it skidded toward the shoulder.

And as it careened off the edge of the road and plunged down an embankment, one stomach-churning thought flashed through his mind.

He'd forgotten to buckle his seat belt.

* * *

Rebecca Matthews stifled a yawn and reached for the cup of coffee in the holder under the dashboard. Grimaced as the cold liquid sluiced down her throat. But she chugged it down anyway. It had been a long day and she needed the caffeine.

She glanced at the clock on the dash. Groaned.

Ten-thirty.

Make that a *very* long day.

Maybe she should have taken her brother up on his offer of a bed for the night when he'd walked her to her car in St. Louis.

Except she'd driven this route a hundred times. And barging in on him just as he and Sam were welcoming a new baby to their family hadn't felt right.

Besides, as she'd assured him, she could make this drive with her eyes closed.

Of course she hadn't meant that literally, but that was close to what she was doing tonight, thanks to the dense, swirling fog.

Tightening her grip on the wheel, she hunched forward and focused on the road. Or what little she could see of it.

So much for her plan to switch to autopilot during the familiar drive. This trek was requiring every ounce of what little energy and concentration she had left. And tomorrow's schedule wouldn't bend to accommodate her late-night arrival home. She'd still have to be up no later than six to prepare for the Friday lunch and dinner crowd at her restaurant. Running out on Rose and Frances today after Brad's call, in the midst of all the Valentine dinner prep, had been bad enough. She couldn't expect them to carry the load tomorrow too.

But she was almost home. Her exit was coming up…if she could see it through the fog.

When the sign at last emerged from the mist, she flipped on her blinker and exhaled. There should be minimal traffic on the secondary highway. Who would be out on such a dismal night, unless a major event like a birth had compelled you to brave the weather?

Maintaining a tight grip on the wheel, she kept close tabs on her surroundings as she drove at a snail's pace, her headlights barely piercing the gloom. Her usual points of reference were invisible, including the homes scattered here and there along the rural road.

She double-checked her gas gauge.

Plenty of fuel to get her home.

Good.

Running out of gas wouldn't be—

She gasped as a figure appeared out of the mist in her headlights, trudging along the edge of the road a handful of feet in front of her car.

She swerved to the left. Jammed on her brakes. Skidded along the slick pavement in the oncoming traffic lane.

When her car finally came to a stop, she looked in her rearview mirror, pulse pounding.

The apparition had been swallowed up in the gloom.

No, not an apparition.

It had been a flesh-and-blood man, wearing a white dress shirt and carrying a suit jacket.

But why had he been walking down the road at this hour of the night in this weather?

Three possibilities flashed through her mind.

He was a lunatic, he was drunk, or he was in trouble.

Her stomach knotted.

She wasn't equipped to deal with any of those situations.

Best plan?

Call 911.

Keeping one eye on her rearview mirror, she guided her car to the shoulder on the right side of the road, confirmed that her doors were locked, and groped in her purse for her phone.

But before she could locate her cell, the man materialized out of the mist again to her left, now walking down the center of the road.

Oh, mercy.

If a car came along, he was a sitting duck.

About the Author

© DeWeesePhotography.com

Irene Hannon is the bestselling, award-winning author of more than sixty-five contemporary romance and romantic suspense novels. She is also a three-time winner of the RITA award—the "Oscar" of romance fiction—from Romance Writers of America, and a member of that organization's elite Hall of Fame.

Her many other awards include National Readers' Choice, Daphne du Maurier, Retailers' Choice, Booksellers' Best, Carol, and Reviewer's Choice from *RT Book Reviews* magazine, which also honored her with a Career Achievement award for her entire body of work. In addition, she is a HOLT medallion winner and a two-time Christy award finalist.

Millions of copies of her books have been sold worldwide, and her novels have been translated into multiple languages.

Irene, who holds a BA in psychology and an MA in journalism, juggled two careers for many years until she gave up her executive corporate communications position with a Fortune 500 company to write full-time. She is happy to say she has no regrets.

A trained vocalist, Irene has sung the leading role in numerous community musical theater productions and is a soloist at her church. She and her husband enjoy traveling, hiking, gardening, and spending time with family. They make their home in Missouri.

To learn more about Irene and her books, visit www.irenehannon.com. She loves to interact with readers on Facebook and is also active on Instagram.

Made in the USA
Las Vegas, NV
10 June 2025

23477562R00121